Track Down Alaska

A Brad Jacobs Thriller

__Book 2__

SCOTT CONRAD

Scott Conrad's "Brad Jacobs Thriller" Series takes retired Force Recon Marine Brad Jacobs and his fellow veterans on dangerous and thrilling international search, rescue and hostage retrieval expeditions. Their missions are to "Track Down" and retrieve innocent victims by facing off against fierce, powerful enemies and extremely challenging conditions.

Enjoy the non-stop action, adventure and mystery with the entire team as they always manage to keep their sense of humor, even during the riskiest of operations. Each book is a complete story on its own.

A Brad Jacobs Thriller Series by Scott Conrad:

TRACK DOWN AFRICA – BOOK 1

TRACK DOWN ALASKA – BOOK 2

TRACK DOWN AMAZON – BOOK 3

TRACK DOWN IRAQ – BOOK 4

TRACK DOWN BORNEO – BOOK 5

TRACK DOWN EL SALVADOR – BOOK 6

TRACK DOWN WYOMING – BOOK 7

TRACK DOWN THAILAND – BOOK 8

Visit the author at: ScottConradBooks.com

"Some people spend an entire lifetime wondering if they made a difference in the world. But, the Marines don't have that problem."

Ronald Reagan, President of the United States; 1985

Table of Contents

CHAPTER ONE

THE CRASH

18 April 1600 hours AKDT

The Piper PA-18-180 Super Cub banked hard to the right as the engine sputtered and quit. The altimeter indicator needle spun wildly as the plane lost altitude, with no place in sight to set down.

Pete Sabrowski, a former Naval Aviator in the Marine Corps, glanced nervously at the Alaskan forest below. It was going to be a tree landing, and that didn't bode well for the passengers or the lightweight fabric and aluminum tube aircraft fuselage. Most pilots considered the Piper the perfect choice for flying in the Alaskan bush, in part because of its ability to take off and land in incredibly short distances.

First generation Cubs were remarkable enough, but the modification that made it the current airplane of choice in the bush was the use of the Lycoming O-360 power plant. A high-lift wing placement design and the powerful one hundred and eighty horsepower engine made the Super Cub especially adaptable to use as either a float plane or a ski plane. This aircraft could take off in as little as two hundred feet.

"Mayday, Mayday!" Sam Henderson, the charter pilot, spoke calmly into the microphone. "I say again, Mayday! This is *Snow Gopher.* Red Piper Super Cub. Engine failure, we're going down. Visibility poor, overshot destination. Best guess is we're just east of Mount Watana. Mayday, Mayday!"

There was no response.

In this part of Alaska, there were no air traffic controllers. Henderson checked to see if the emergency location transmitter (ELT) light was blinking. He thumped the switch once hard and the red light started flashing. There was an FAA monitoring station in Talkeetna, but if they were responding Henderson couldn't hear them. There was no other response.

Normally bush pilots listen for distress calls and respond or retransmit if they're near enough to pick up the SOS. Sam Henderson mentally berated himself for his poor choice in not turning back to Talkeetna when the weather went bad so quickly. He had known better than to chance it, but the Stephan Lake Lodge hop was a short one and he had flown it a thousand times.

It had seemed to him at the time no riskier to continue on to the lodge than to try to return to Talkeetna. Besides, there was a sweet little redhead at the lodge who usually made room in her bed for him when he landed there.

Visibility had gotten progressively worse and his chronometer told him he had missed Stephan Lake. They had been flying too long. He explained to Pete Sabrowski that he had overshot their destination and began a slow turn back to the southeast, dropping to the lowest level he dared, looking for a familiar landmark. That's when the carburetor had iced over and the engine sputtered to a stop.

"Shit, we're going in!" he barked, and initiated the Mayday call. He didn't bother to tell Pete to prepare for a hard landing. From their conversation earlier he had learned that Pete was an experienced pilot himself, though his experience in the Arctic seemed limited. He left it up to Pete to warn the other passenger, who was curled into the cramped rear seat behind them.

From the small makeshift third seat in the cargo area Charlie Dawkins began to sweat as he watched the trees getting closer at an alarming rate. At under a thousand feet, he could clearly see snow and ice everywhere. And the trees—weird, thin trees and tall. There was no place between them to land the plane. The only thing that looked remotely feasible was the frozen surface of a river, and it looked as if the pilot was trying to glide toward that. Charlie thought it unlikely that they would reach it based on their current glide path. He was partly right.

"This is it!" Sam called out just before all of them were slammed forward in the cockpit.

The plane clipped the tops of several of the thin fir trees and then skidded sideways as it slammed onto the frozen surface of the river. The ice held, and the aircraft seemed to slide forever. The left side landing gear collapsed with the force of the impact, and the wing broke off on that side when they slid into the riverbank. The wing tank ruptured, exploding in an enormous fireball.

Charlie kept his head tucked down between his knees, and he didn't see the billowing black smoke until it was all over. The aircraft finally came to rest on the right bank of the river.

Pete could smell the burning aviation fuel and knew immediately that there was no time to lose. They needed to get out of the craft as quickly as possible.

The only door in the small plane was on the passenger side, and it looked flimsy as hell, mostly shattered Plexiglas. Pete managed to get his seatbelt unfastened and slammed his back against the small access door, tumbling out on his back onto the ice. Charlie scrambled through headfirst and landed on his shoulder, wincing at the pain.

It was Charlie's first trip to the Arctic, and he was surprised at the consistency of the snow on top of the river ice. It felt dry and powdery, and he had the inane thought that making a snowball out of the stuff would be damned near impossible.

Pete didn't bother to check on Charlie. The pilot was still in the plane, slumped forward and unconscious. He clambered back through the shattered frame of the door and fumbled for the pilot's seatbelt latch. Smoke billowed from the fire, and Pete choked on it, his eyes watering profusely as he maneuvered Sam Henderson's inert body out of the cockpit and into the frigid air. Coughing and hacking, he dragged Henderson a safe distance away from the wreckage while Charlie helped as best he could, ignoring the pain in his shoulder.

Henderson was out cold, and Pete was concerned about the nasty red lump on the pilot's forehead.

"Is he all right?" Charlie asked, his voice hoarse in the chilled air.

"Can't tell," Pete answered. "He took a hell of a lick on the forehead when we hit. Last I saw he was still trying to manhandle the bird over those last trees. I don't think he had time to brace himself before we hit." There was respect in his voice. The pilot had put his aircraft and his passengers first, ignoring his own safety in the process. He glanced back at the wreckage, noticing that the fire had gone out . . . at least for the moment.

"Are you okay, Charlie?"

"Yeah, but I'm gonna be sore as hell for a few days."

"I don't want to leave this guy, even for a minute, right now. How about you climb back in there and see if you can find his first aid kit, and then toss out any survival gear you can locate?"

"Will do," Charlie said, slowly getting to his feet. His shoulder hurt like hell, but it didn't feel like anything was broken.

The outer skin of the Super Cub was the heaviest weight Dacron fabric available, and even though it was coated with polyurethane it was highly flammable. There was extensive fire damage on the pilot's side of the aircraft, but the rest seemed to be intact. It was apparent that the other wing tank had ruptured and the smell of aviation fuel sucked the oxygen out of their lungs. Pete didn't have to tell him to be careful. It would only take one small spark to turn the wreckage into a funeral pyre for Charlie.

Pete watched Charlie crawl into the wreckage and then turned his attention back to Henderson. The pilot looked bad. His face had gone gray and there was that swollen red bump on his forehead. His breathing was shallow and rapid. Moving the man as little as possible, Pete began to treat him for shock, but as he loosened the pilot's clothing the man gave a bubbly, rattling gasp and stopped breathing.

"You can stop looking for the first aid kit," Pete called out. "He's gone...." He sniffed at the frigid air. "You'd better toss out the guns and the survival gear. It smells like the fuel leak is getting worse."

Pete's rib cage hurt like hell, but necessity kept him going despite the pain. He stood slowly and walked toward the wreckage to take the gun cases Charlie passed through the gaping hole where the door had been.

"You sure he's dead?" Charlie asked as he passed a small bag of ammunition through the opening.

Pete gave the man a strange look. "I've seen enough dead people that I can say with relative certainty that, yeah, he's gone."

Charlie tossed a duffel bag through the opening onto the ice, and Pete heard a muffled "Whooomp!" when a spark struck by the metal grommet on the duffel bag hit the thin film of gas on the ice beneath the wing.

"Get out!" he screamed, reaching through the opening for Charlie's outstretched arm and dragging him to safety just as another, smaller explosion happened.

The men lay on the cold ground watching the oranges and reds of the fire. "Jesus, that was close," Charlie panted. "Thanks buddy."

Pete dragged the gun and ammunition cases away from the blaze as the flames licked at what remained of the fabric covering the plane. There was nothing they could do but watch, so he absently busied himself by taking out the specially modified M-14 that had always been his weapon of choice for hunting. He'd done the gunsmithing himself, and he was consistently making refinements to the weapon, which was already the finest hunting rifle he'd ever used. The lightweight composite stock and the bull barrel were the two most obvious modifications, but a closer examination of the weapon revealed a myriad of other changes.

Charlie unpacked and loaded his own rifle as the two of them watched the flames devour the rest of their gear.

Pete had already reached survival mode, and as he absently fiddled with his rifle his mind focused on their situation. There was no question that they were in deep shit. Henderson had overshot the area he was personally familiar with, and he had very little idea of where they were. He had no map, and he doubted that the aircraft radio would be in functioning condition when the fire finally went out. He didn't know if anyone had received Henderson's Mayday and he had no idea whether the emergency location transmitter had actually worked.

Nevertheless, he knew that it would be better to make themselves as comfortable as possible and stay by the wreckage until someone came for them. To stay with the bigger search target only made sense. Regardless, the guns would be essential to their survival. The predators in this neck of the woods were fearsome, and they were coming off a long, cold winter. They would be hungry.

He didn't know how much of Charlie's experience was firsthand and how much had come from a book. The hard core of Pete's character was solidifying. Once a Marine, always a Marine.

Semper Fidelis applied to being faithful to oneself as much as it meant being faithful to the Corps and to other Marines. He had work to do. There was firewood to be collected, a shelter to be built, and by the time those tasks were done, the wreckage should be cool enough to scrounge through it to see what they could scavenge. He didn't have time to waste.

It was late in the afternoon and dark was fast approaching. The temperatures would drop by twenty degrees or more in this remote part of Alaska by nightfall. Pete shrugged off the pain and stood up to begin the numerous tasks he knew had to be accomplished.

WITNESS

The man stood on a hillock in the Susitna River Valley, on land the U.S. Government claimed as the Nelchina Public Use Area. This part of the Nelchina area was controlled by the Order of Phineas, a splinter group of the Aryan Nations. The group was composed of several hundred men and women living in the Susitna River Valley. They had relocated here after being run out of Washington State a couple of years before by political infighting in the extremist organization.

The Order of Phineas disputed the revisionist policies of the new leadership within the Aryan Nations and refused to acknowledge the ZOG (Zionist Occupied Government) or its claim on the land. There was gold here, and the man and his followers were collecting it by panning for it and by placer mining.

They followed the streams and rivers northward seeking the mother lode, the source of all the nuggets they'd found. The group had long since stopped collecting flakes and grains, and the nuggets were getting larger and more common.

The members of the Order of Phineas were tough, experienced people; many were former military, highly trained in weapons use and military maneuvers. In addition to their work mining gold, they spent several hours a day maintaining their readiness and training. There was no place for slackers here.

If no one came snooping around, they would soon have accumulated enough gold to carry the war to the enemy, proponents of miscegenation, homosexuality, and desegregation—those who would pervert the natural order of things. Until they were ready, though, they needed to keep their presence and location secret as well as their purchases of weapons and future plans for nationwide expansion and terrorist attacks.

As if the heavens had read his thoughts, the man's reverie was interrupted by a low flying bush plane, a red one, in the skies above him. His eyes narrowed as he focused on the aircraft. It was flying incredibly slowly and seemed to be losing altitude. Anger rose in him at the intrusion.

The group could not afford to be spotted, and there were flumes scattered about the streams and rivers, work crews busily collecting gold nuggets from their beds. He hoped one of the sentries might have sense enough to shoot at the aircraft and chase it away.

As if fate were reading his mind, the man heard the engine sputter and watched the bush plane begin a steep descent. It was going to crash, though it would come down miles away. And it was far too near nightfall to mount an expedition, even though the man and his people knew the land well.

He shrugged. If the passengers survived, they wouldn't get very far, and if they did he had nothing to fear. His own people were expert skiers and they could locate any survivors the next day or the day after.

Just as he reached one of his security crews, he caught a distant muffled explosion and looked back over his shoulder to see a large plume of black smoke rising into the air. He smiled. Maybe the crash had done his work for him. It didn't matter. A good leader leaves nothing to chance.

CHAPTER TWO

BAD NEWS

Dallas, Texas 19 April

Brad Jacobs awoke from a deep sleep at 0230 Dallas time to the sound of his phone ringing. It was Mason Ving, his best friend and former Force Recon sergeant.

"What's up?" he asked in a voice sleep-laden and groggy.

"I've got some bad news," Ving said hesitantly. "Pete and Charlie never made it to their destination."

Brad knew that Pete Sabrowski, another friend and retired Force Recon Marine, was supposed to be at Stephan Lake Hunting Lodge in the Alaskan wilderness on his annual bear hunting trip, along with Charlie Dawkins, who'd recently started dating Brad's cousin, Jessica.

"What do you mean they didn't make it?" Brad asked, suddenly wide awake and more alert.

"They left Talkeetna on schedule and were due to arrive at the lodge at Stephan Lake at 1600 hours yesterday. Their plane never showed."

"Has there been any contact at all?"

"None from what I can tell so far. The lodge manager called me."

"Was Pete flying?"

"No. They had a local pilot, a real hotshot with a helluva reputation as a bush pilot."

Brad remembered Pete talking about how much he enjoyed this trip every year. He'd said it was as far off the map as you could get and still be in the good old US of A. The Talkeetna Mountains and the

Susitna River Valley lay approximately halfway between Anchorage to the south and Fairbanks to the north and nearly halfway between Denali National Park and Wrangell-St. Elias National Park to the east and west. If you wanted to get lost, you couldn't find a better place.

"Have they located a position from the ELT?" Brad asked.

"I don't think so. The manager didn't have a lot of information yet. There's no report of anyone locating wreckage."

Brad's mind slipped into overdrive, evaluating what he knew for certain about the area. "What's the weather like?"

"Nasty right now, spring snowstorm. That's one reason why the manager was worried. He said it's possible that the pilot just encountered rough weather and set it down somewhere to wait out the storm. He says those bush pilots know where all the cabins are up there, and it's not uncommon for them to set down and wait out bad weather; but their last reported position put them over public lands. Nobody lives out that way."

"Any ranger stations?"

"Brad, I just don't know. I called you as soon as I got off the phone with the manager of the lodge."

Brad understood the Arctic well, and he knew that anyone stranded and unprepared, even in early spring conditions, during which the temperatures usually ranged in the low teens to the mid-thirties in April, only lasted about forty-eight hours even if they were not injured. Pete was well trained in arctic survival, but Brad had no idea what kind of survival gear Pete might have had with him. The lodge generally provided the gear, including the baggy parkas that retained body heat even in the lowest of temperatures. Time would be critical if Pete were in a jam.

"Who's leading the search and rescue?"

"Alaska State Troopers," Ving replied sourly. They both knew the troopers were stretched far too thin in the wilds of Alaska.

"Did you call Jessica and tell her yet?"

"No, not yet."

"Prep a mission, Ving. How soon can we be wheels up?"

"Who do you want?"

"We're going to need our own pilot, just in case. See if you can reach Tom Riggins." He hesitated a moment. "Go ahead and get Jared and Jessica too."

"Jessica?" Ving asked. "Why in the hell do you want to take Jessica?"

Jessica was Brad's younger cousin and not someone he had ever wanted on a mission. It wasn't that the slender blonde wasn't competent;

Ving knew for a fact that the beautiful, athletic woman was an adventuress with mad skills. He'd seen her in action. Her beauty could distract from her capabilities, but it still seemed odd as hell that Brad would want to take her to Alaska, of all places. Ving had trained there extensively, and he hated the place. It was damned pretty in the movies and on television, but it was no place for a sun-loving black man.

Since retiring as a Force Recon Marine four years before, Brad had made a living as a seeker. Even though he'd just turned thirty-eight he stayed in peak physical condition. He worked out religiously. He possessed a forceful look of self-confidence in his piercing green eyes that came from his years of experience dealing with life-and-death situations. With his short, blond hair, white skin, and square jaw, women often told him he looked like a movie star, but he never took them seriously. He enjoyed plenty of short-term girlfriends, but he never managed to stay at home long enough to form a long-term relationship even if he'd wanted one.

He was dedicated to his work. Respect, honor, and hard work were more than just words to him; they were a way of life. He liked the feeling of really making a difference. He was known by his friends as someone with incredible resourcefulness and integrity, and he carried a well-known reputation for believing that justice was something everyone deserved.

Often he worked as a bounty hunter, and when the money was right, he tracked down and located missing persons who had vanished in dangerous countries that conventional law enforcement agencies shied away from. When he took one of these latter missions, he always enlisted the help of selected men he had previously served with and trusted. Ving was always first on his list, the two of them went way back, and they had been on missions with each other many times.

The others were professionals he knew—he could count on them. Pete was one of those men, and the best all-around pilot Brad had ever met. He recruited Pete frequently for his private operations. Brad made a point of taking a pilot on every job, even if their basic plan didn't require one, and Pete could fly anything that moved through the air. Aside from being a handy fellow to have his back in a fight, he was good insurance.

Besides working as a bounty hunter, Brad had also worked recently as a hostage retrieval expert for international corporations, rescuing high-level executives who had been abducted for ransom in foreign countries. He was earning a worldwide reputation as a man who could track down anyone anywhere and bring them back in one piece. It made no difference if it were a dangerous felon who skipped bail or an innocent victim who had been kidnapped halfway around the world, Brad put everything he had into every job he accepted.

That was something he learned at a very young age from his father. It had served him well.

"Why Jessica?" Ving repeated.

"Because she'll insist on showing up anyway," Brad responded. "Charlie Dawkins is her newest flame, and I'd rather have her close by where I can keep an eye on her than have her running around the wilds of Alaska on her own . . . and you know as well as I do that she would do exactly that if I tried to exclude her from this. Hell, she might even be useful; she's a better skier than I am." He thought for a moment. "On second thought, I'll call Jessica," he said quietly. "You call everybody else."

A woman with a spirit of adventure like Jessica was not likely to sit idly by and wait for someone to find her missing boyfriend. Brad knew she would end up right in the middle of things if he didn't take her along. If he told her to stay at home and wait for him to call, she'd be on the next commercial flight to Talkeetna and he'd have no way of stopping her.

He'd rescued her enough times to anticipate her reactions.

"What kind of weapons and how many?" Ving asked. "We're only talking Alaska this time. It should be a little less rowdy than Africa was. Do you just want me to take hunting rifles?"

"Ving, you know better than to ask me that."

Ving smiled. He already knew what Brad's response would be before he'd asked the question. One thing they both learned as Marines was to always be prepared, to anticipate the unexpected, particularly when it came to challenges and potential adversaries. Readiness was their stock in trade. Brad never went looking for trouble, but somehow it always seemed to find him. His standing rule was that he always went fully armed with military weapons on every mission, even if it was only a simple search and rescue on American soil.

"Okay," Ving said. "I'll give you an update at 0600. We should be ready to go wheels up by 0800, provided we can get the others up and moving by then."

"Ving?"

"Yeah, Brad?"

"Use the 'War Chest' credit card for whatever you need."

"Roger that, Brad!"

The 'War Chest' credit card was for use in situations where Brad was footing the bill for an op or when they were awaiting funds from a client. It had come in handy on numerous occasions, and Ving carried one of the plastic cards in his wallet. It was a measure of how much Brad trusted him.

As Brad hung up the phone the enormity of the situation struck him. Alaska was one of the most dangerous environments on Earth, even in early spring. Perilous terrain, extreme temperatures, and savage, hungry animals coming off a long cold winter were only the most obvious of perils. Even for an experienced arctic survivalist the risks were staggering.

Cold injuries such as frostbite were the norm rather than the exception, and while most people were not aware of it, heat stroke was more common than hypothermia, because people who didn't know better tended to overdress for the cold. The secret to staying warm enough to survive in the Arctic was not the amount of clothes one wore but the amount of dead air space trapped in the clothing and keeping the dry, biting wind from one's exposed skin.

Dehydration was another unexpected gift of the Arctic. Dry, cold air sucked the moisture from the mouth, nostrils, and lungs at an alarming rate and people who tried to use snowmelt for water replenishment were in for a rude shock. A five-gallon bucket of dry, powdery snow yielded perhaps a half a teacup of drinkable water, and pure snowmelt leached the minerals from the body, which made it worthless, actually worse than worthless, for rehydration. Melting snow for water in the Arctic was an exercise in futility and frustration.

Brad had hated the U.S. Army's Northern Warfare Training Course at Fort Greeley, Alaska, where the Corps had seen fit to send him, but he had gained an enormous amount of knowledge at the school, and he'd been provided the opportunity to put it into actual practice. It had come in handy before and it would come in doubly handy now.

Pete was not just a Marine he had served with. Pete was one of his best friends, and Brad was the kind of man who didn't hesitate to act when one of his friends was in trouble. No matter what the cost, nothing could keep him from helping a friend in real trouble.

He knew less about Charles Dawkins. From the time he had learned that Charlie was dating his favorite cousin Jessica Paul, it had been Brad's intention to run a background check on the man, although he knew Jessica would be mad as hell when she found out about it. He'd never found the time, and it hadn't seemed really important because Pete had taken to the man right away. Pete had good instincts, which Brad trusted almost as much as he trusted his own, but there was something about Charlie that bothered him, and he just didn't know exactly what.

JESSICA

Brad didn't call Jessica. He dressed quickly, grabbed his arctic bag from the hall closet, and drove to her apartment. The lights were out when he arrived at the plush Dallas building. He dreaded waking her up this time of the morning with bad news, but he dreaded even more trying to explain why he hadn't woken her. If he waited until daylight to tell her, she'd probably take his scalp. He often thought of her as his little cousin, but at times like these he had to force himself to remember her facing the *Séléka* in the Congo with a rifle in her hand and an expression of cool professionalism on her pretty face. She was, in fact, one very cool, competent warrior in the face of hostile fire.

He forced himself to calm down and knocked firmly on her door. To his surprise, she answered it quickly, wearing an old, ratty looking terrycloth robe that she had worn as far back as he could remember. He knew she had plenty of money from a trust fund and that her father, his uncle Jack, gave her an allowance as well, in addition to her income as a successful treasure hunter. She drove a brand new Porsche, and it seemed to him odd that she would keep wearing such a ratty old robe at home when she could afford anything she wanted.

"What are you doing here in the middle of the night?" she asked. She knew something was wrong and she stood in the doorway without moving or asking him inside.

"Jessica . . . " he started.

"It's Charlie, isn't it?" She wasn't crying, but he could tell she was close to tears.

"Let me in, Jessica, and I'll tell you all about it."

She seemed startled, and then she composed herself. She opened the door and indicated the kitchen table. "Sit down. I'll make us some coffee and then you can tell me."

He watched as she went through her coffee ritual carefully, rinsing the coffee pot with cold water, meticulously measuring out the proper amount of beans and grinding them thoroughly in a deluxe grinder that must have cost the equivalent of a month's salary for a private in the Corps. She poured the water into a fancy copper coffee maker and removed delicate looking china cups and saucers from a cabinet while she waited for the brew to filter into the glass coffee pot. When it was done, she poured carefully and brought both cups and saucers to the table where she sat across from him. She took a sip, as did he, and then clasped her hands in front of her.

"Please. Just tell me he isn't dead." Her eyes were pleading silently.

"We think the plane he and Pete were in went down in Alaska. They never reached Stephan Lake Lodge. Ving's alerting a crew and trying to get more information right now. I know the Alaska State Troopers are in charge of rescue operations, Jessica, but I swear I don't know anything else."

"You're going up there?"

"Of course, and I've come to pick you up and take you with me." She was out of the chair and hugging him tightly before he could even take another sip of coffee. He hadn't seen any tears, but he could feel the wetness on his neck.

"Thank you," she whispered.

"Don't thank me," Brad said drily. "You'll change your mind when we get there. It's colder than a bucket of penguin poop up there right now."

"Couldn't be any worse than the heat in Africa when we were there last summer." She pulled back from him, seeming more in control of her emotions and with no tears visible. "I guess I'd better get packing."

"Don't pack a lot and make sure everything is bulky and oversized. Remember that dead air space is the best insulator you can have. We'll get parkas and vapor barrier boots up there."

"I remember how to dress in the Arctic," she said primly. "Remember? I had the best teacher in the world."

He grinned. He'd taken her on a cruise to Alaska when she turned eighteen, and they visited a ski resort when the cruise ship had finally docked. Just then something clicked inside his mind like the last tumbler settling into place in a lock. The robe she was wearing had been his gift to her, something to wear in the cabin on the cruise ship because the one she brought with her was a peignoir and he'd felt uncomfortable being around her when she was wearing the flimsy garment.

Jessica saw that he was staring at her robe. "Yeah, it's the same old one."

"My god, Jessica, you ought to throw that ratty old thing out and get yourself something decent to wear."

"Nope," she said with a brilliant smile. "I'm keeping this one. After all, someone I cherish gave it to me." She bent to kiss his nose and then she turned and walked to her bedroom to pack.

Cherish. Brad felt a lump rise in his throat.

CHAPTER THREE

MISSION PREP

Day 2 0330 hours CDST

Ving's first call when planning a mission for Brad was usually to Hank Guzman, an old friend. Ving had known Hank for over twenty years, and knew that Hank had worked on mission logistics for the military, the CIA, and two other "didn't exist" government agencies he was not allowed to talk about. Hank was semi-retired, but he still had all the right contacts in all the right places. The man was the best Black Ops logistics specialist Ving had ever known, and was still a tremendous resource.

Usually Ving preferred to work backwards, using completion of the mission as a starting point and planning everything back to the initial departure time so he could ensure that they had taken everything they would need along with them. This time, as so often before, he didn't have that luxury so he relied on Brad's SOP (standard operating procedure).

When any military unit works together for any length of time, they develop SOPs, which they use as checklists to save time in getting an operation off the ground. There was an SOP for air travel, including procedures for transporting weapons legally on commercial flights, another for waterborne operations, and so on. Ving only had the sketchiest outline in his head concerning this rescue mission, but he had multiple SOPs that should cover almost anything, and he dove into his planning headfirst.

Ving reached for the phone and dialed Hank's number. It rang three times and then he heard a click, followed by Hank's recorded voice. Ving left a terse message. After a few minutes, he dialed another number, Hank's beeper, and then punched in his own phone number followed by 9-1-1. That should get Hank's attention.

Ving's next call was to Jared Smoot. Jared was a highly decorated and retired Force Recon Marine sniper. He was a member of Brad's regular team and had played a key role in most of their previous private missions. On their last mission to Africa to rescue Jessica, he took a bullet in the shoulder. It had been several months and Jared was fully healed but had not been on a mission since. The phone rang four times and then went to voicemail. Ving left him an urgent message and then did the same on Jared's beeper, adding 9-1-1 at the end just as he had with Hank.

Two strikes, not a good omen. Ving turned his mind back to his planning. He knew that he and Brad both kept different duffel bags stashed in their homes, bags packed for different climates so that they could leave at a moment's notice. Ving had labeled his bags A, B, C, and D. The A bag was for tropical climates, B for deserts, C for a temperate climate, and D was for cold weather. Clothing and cold weather gear settled, his mind turned to weapons.

They would have to travel light in the likely event that they ended up on foot in the Alaska high country. He made a mental note to contact David Hansen at the Northern Warfare Training Center annex at Black Rapids, near Fort Greeley, about getting an *ahkio*. That word always sounded so strange to Ving until he looked it up and learned it was a Finnish word. It was derived from the Lappish word akja, for an open, canoe-shaped sled of Nordic design. Ving was like that. He always had to know the meaning of everything.

The *ahkio* had been adopted by the military as a way of enabling ground troops to transport essential survival equipment too bulky or heavy to backpack in the extreme conditions of cold weather warfare. The *ahkio* currently in use was constructed of light wood, aluminum or fiberglass and weighed nearly twenty-five pounds. It could carry one to two hundred pounds of gear and could be pulled easily by a man on skis or snowshoes.

David was an old friend from the Special Operations community, and he not only had access to the equipment they would need, he'd be happy to help them. Pete had saved his ass a couple of times, extracting him from some pretty intense situations in Afghanistan and Iraq.

Ving decided that everyone could use their own personal weapons, prototype M4A1s equipped with bull barrels and suppressors. He'd picked them up through another friend when the team had gone to the Central African Republic to find Jessica and bring her home. Jared carried his personal M40A5 sniper rifle and all of them carried M45 MEUSOC .45 caliber pistols.

He made a note to bring three extra rifles from his personal collection, one for Jessica and a couple spares. A handful of spare ordnance they probably would never need could be carried in a satchel. They were unlikely to need hand grenades, but flash-bangs might come in handy if they needed to chase away a grizzly or a pack of wolves that hunted in the interior.

The next item on his agenda was transportation. Alaska was actually one of the easiest states to transport weapons into. They loved tourists and they absolutely welcomed hunters. The easiest method of getting the weapons into Alaska was to have the team pack and register them as luggage. The ordnance satchel would be concealed in a crate with the gear they wouldn't have time to acquire in Alaska.

They could fly from Dallas to Anchorage direct on a commercial flight or a charter, which would really make it easier to get everything up there if they happened to get lucky and find one headed there with empty seats. That would actually be easier than it sounded. Texas was full of avid hunters eager to hunt the wilds of Alaska. A connecting flight to the small town of Talkeetna should carry them through the next step of their journey. He couldn't book transportation for the last leg of the trip until he knew for sure exactly who was going and acquired more information regarding where Pete's plane had gone down.

He was hopeful that Hank would be able to arrange transport for the last leg. To Ving's way of thinking, the last leg was a no-brainer. They needed a chopper because they had no idea where they might have to set down, but they could be pretty well assured there'd be no airfield.

Ving still hadn't heard from Jared, so he called Tom Riggins as Brad had requested. Riggins was another retired Force Recon Marine, not one of the guys that Brad used on a regular basis, but nevertheless he was an expert tracker and specially trained in cold weather survival. They'd used him a couple of times but it had been a while and Ving was not sure if he could reach him on such short notice. As Ving dialed Riggins' number, he recalled that the man was also a qualified pilot, though he didn't know if Riggins' flight experience included time in the Arctic.

To Ving's surprise Tom picked up on the first ring.

"Hello Ving," he said with a welcoming voice.

"Hi Tom, I wasn't sure if you'd pick up at this time of the morning," Ving replied.

"Are you kidding me? There is only one reason you'd be calling me at this hour and we both know what that is. I'm bored, buddy, I'm bored as hell and I'm ready. Just tell me when and where."

Ving laughed. He understood that. Most retired Marines were always looking for some excitement, and nothing got their blood pumping better than a mission with a purpose, even if it was just a search and rescue mission.

"Alaska, somewhere north of Talkeetna and southwest of Fort Greeley. How're your skiing skills these days?"

"So-so," Tom replied, "but I prefer the new style lightweight magnesium snowshoes when I'm pulling an ahkio." Tom looked to be built like a bull and massively strong. Ving didn't think the man ever laid hands on anything he couldn't pick up. The new style snowshoes he was referring to were easier to use than the older model, and they possessed teeth on the bottom similar to the crampons used by ice climbers.

"I've still got to book a flight, but I expect we'll depart out of DFW (Dallas/Fort Worth International Airport) around 0800. When I checked earlier, they still had quite a few seats open. I'll call you back with the exact flight information—and don't forget your weapon."

"Affirmative, I'll be ready and waiting for your call."

Ving dialed Jared's number again in the hopes of catching the man, but whatever Jared might be doing he either couldn't or wouldn't pick up the phone. He'd never had any trouble reaching the sniper before, and he was beginning to worry about him.

There was no time for that now, he'd promised to get the arrangements done and get back to Brad by 0600 and he was running out of time.

The number to the Alaska State Troopers' office in Talkeetna was scribbled on a scratch pad beside his desk phone, and Ving quickly punched in the numbers. Trooper Lieutenant Ben Robinson must have been sitting right next to his phone because he answered before the first ring finished. He was the same trooper who'd left a voicemail for Ving a few minutes earlier while he was on the phone with Tom. Apparently, Pete had listed Ving as an emergency contact on the waiver form he'd signed when he'd hired the charter to take him and Charlie to Stephan Lake Lodge.

"Robinson!" he barked.

"This is Mason Ving. You called earlier regarding Pete Sabrowski. Can you give me an update on the status of your search and rescue mission?" Ving asked.

"We're still waiting for sunrise," Robinson replied. "We could put the search plane in the air, but it wouldn't do us a hell of a lot of good."

Ving controlled his temper as best he could. *Plane? One plane?*

"We normally get thirteen to fourteen hours of sunshine a day up here this time of year, but we've got whiteout conditions up around Mount Watana and the weather has all aircraft grounded right now. We're monitoring the weather situation very closely and we'll have the plane up as soon as the weather permits.

"The good news is that we've received an intermittent signal from their ELT; the bad news is that they appear to be way off their planned flight path. The pings we did receive seem to be coming from up near Mount Watana. That's at a much higher altitude than Stephan Lake and north and east of it as well. With this weather front, that's not encouraging."

"How could the ELT be sending out 'intermittent' signals? And why are you sending up just one plane?" Ving was trying to keep the exasperation he felt out of his voice, but he knew he wasn't succeeding very well.

"Mr. Ving, this is Alaska. I have four troopers stationed here in Talkeetna to cover twenty-five thousand square miles. I'm one of those four troopers, and I have a single pilot to go with my single plane." The lieutenant was trying to control his own temper, as much for his embarrassment at the scarcity of his resources as at the intemperance of this yokel from the lower forty-eight who simply did not understand the enormity of the task ahead of them.

He took a deep breath and continued. "The bush pilots up here have a sort of loose association of their own, and they'll be up and searching as soon as the weather permits. Every one of them knows that could be them out there waiting for help."

"Sorry," Ving said, meaning it. He appreciated what it was like to be at the sharp end of the stick with inadequate resources and an inhuman task in front of him. It was a condition that Marines faced on a regular basis.

"There are a few other groups that will be helping as well, but it's going to take time to get them here and get them deployed. They operate out of

Anchorage, and that's a hell of a long way from here."

"Look, I was out of line and I'm sorry. Pete is an old Marine buddy and he's saved my ass more times than I can count. I'm pretty stressed about being so helpless."

"You guys are Marines?"

"Force Recon. Retired, now."

"I was with the Third Battalion, Fifth Marines in Helmand Province back in 2010," Robinson said.

"The Dark Horse," Ving muttered approvingly. The $3/5^{th}$ had seen some nasty action in Helmand Province that year, taking more than a few casualties.

"Get some!" Robinson responded automatically. The phrase was the unit's motto.

"Once a Marine, always a Marine," Ving said. There was a moment of silent bonding between the two men, separated physically by many miles but together in spirit at that moment. The bond between Marines is mysterious, incredibly strong, and only truly understood by other Marines. "Semper Fi, brother."

"Listen," Robinson said, "I swear I'll have someone in the air as soon as the weather clears. I can even get him up before daylight if it's possible because it will take him at least an hour to get up in the area. I've got to warn you, though, unless we get more transmissions from his ELT, it's going to be hard as hell to find him."

"I still don't understand how that could happen," Ving said. "I thought those things were indestructible." There was silence on the other end of the phone, and Ving had a gut feeling that something was being left unsaid. He let it go.

"We'll be up there tomorrow," Ving said. "I'll call and let you know what time to expect us."

"That'll be great," Robinson said, but the warmth was gone from his voice. "We'll have the light on for you." He hung up the phone and stared at the old-fashioned rotary device that was all he had to communicate with. Cell phones weren't worth a damn in the North Country because there were no cell towers. Most communications were conducted over CB radios and aircraft radios.

Robinson suspected that he knew very well why the ELT signal wasn't getting out, and it wasn't likely to be caused by damage to the device. There was something else that would keep the signal from broadcasting, something he didn't really want to dwell on—electronic jamming.

No sooner had Ving set his handset down than the phone rang.

"Ving! It's me, Hank."

"What do you know, Hank?"

"Got a couple of things for you, Ving. First, none of the commercial airlines are gonna let you bring a combat load of ammunition in for 'hunting' so I've arranged to have your ammo delivered to Talkeetna as soon as the weather clears. All I need to get from you is the caliber and quantity."

Ving answered him quickly, specifying the quantities of 5.56 mm rounds for the M4A1s, .45 caliber rounds for the pistols, and .50 caliber ammo for Jared's Barrett. Hank repeated the calibers and quantities verbatim and Ving confirmed them.

"The other thing is that I can arrange transport from Talkeetna by chopper with no problem at all. Hell, I can rent one with a pilot familiar with the area as cheap as I can without. There's a Bell 212 Twin available at a reasonable cost."

Ving grinned at the phone. The Bell 212 Twin was based on the Bell 205 Iroquois, the civilian version of the classic "Huey," but was powered by a pair of PT6 turbines driving a single gearbox, instead of the single engine of the 205. The second turbine gave the chopper the ability to fly at higher temperatures and at higher altitudes. It was as familiar to Ving as his own pickup truck.

CHAPTER FOUR

CURIOSITY

Day 2 0540 hours CDST

Brad fidgeted irritably, going so far as to turn on his stereo to a country music station. Tim McGraw's heartfelt voice was soulfully singing "If You're Reading This", which didn't do much to lift Brad's spirits at all. Unable to contain himself and wait until 0600, at 0540 he turned down the stereo and called Ving. Something about this mission troubled him, but he only had part of an idea what it might be.

Ving picked upon the first ring. "I was just getting ready to call you," he said.

"There's one more thing I need you to do."

"What's that?"

"Run a full background check on Charlie Dawkins."

"Why?" Ving asked.

"I'm not sure, Ving. Just do it, okay?"

Ving recognized the determined tone in Brad's voice. It was a tone that he only heard when Brad was going to get his way, and his friend would either explain the reason why later or he wouldn't.

"Okay, but I may not have the results you want before we go wheels-up."

"Just do what you can, buddy." There was a brief pause. "How's the mission shaping up?"

"I haven't been able to reach Jared yet. I've left two messages, but he hasn't returned my calls."

"I'll run him down," Brad replied. "Jessica's ready to go. What about the rest of the team and transport?"

"We're good to go. Commercial flight out of Dallas-Fort Worth at 0815 hours. We've got a one-hour layover in Seattle and then it's on to Ted Stevens Anchorage International Airport. We should arrive at around 1300 hours local time. From there we'll catch a connector flight from Anchorage to Talkeetna. I went ahead and booked a seat for Jared, and I caught up with Tom Riggins in case I couldn't reach Jared."

"That's just as well. Tom went through N.W.T.C. with me. He's good in the cold and he's a hell of a tracker. Good man in a firefight too." Brad paused again. "And then what?"

"I'm still working on that, Brad, but Hank said it's just as cheap to rent a chopper with a pilot in Talkeetna as it is to rent a chopper by itself. It seems they don't want to rent out their choppers to pilots that don't have local experience. Hank is making a few calls and I should have something set up before we leave."

"That's good enough for me, brother. I'll meet you at the airport at 0730."

Brad hung up the phone without waiting for Ving's response. They'd been close friends for so long that they had developed a kind of mental link that enabled them to finish each other's sentences. People who overheard their conversations were frequently confused because they had to say so little to each other to communicate their thoughts. The resultant conversations were often indecipherable to anyone else.

One thing he always counted on was knowing everything possible concerning all the people involved in a mission before it began. That was the main reason he always used retired Marines to form his teams, men he served with. He and Ving had saved each other's lives more times than he could remember. They'd seen combat together many times when they were in the Marines. And they'd been on enough rescue and recovery missions, that they'd had to intervene to save one another. Their shared memories were etched in blood, blood they had spilled in the deserts and mountains of Iraq and Afghanistan, especially during the infamous Second Battle of Fallujah.

In those days, Ving had been his gunny and had always been the one in command. Now that Brad was in charge, Ving tendered him the same cooperation and respect that Brad had previously shown Ving. They were the closest of friends, both on and off the battlefield.

Brad poured another mug of the steaming fragrant coffee from Jessica's pot as he stared at her. She had everything packed and she was fully dressed, lying on the sofa with one hand flung over her eyes, her hair spilling over a pillow onto one of the sofa cushions.

She had always been more than just a cousin to Brad. Jessica was more like the little sister he'd never had—a sister who always seemed to get herself into trouble. Brad and his mother had spent part of his childhood living with Jessica and her dad. So they'd always been close as siblings. With her long, blonde hair, brilliant blue eyes, and firm, athletic body, she looked like a swimsuit model, but she packed a great deal of muscle into that slender figure. He grinned.

She was an adventure junkie, couldn't get enough of it. Treasure hunts were her weakness as well as her business, and Brad had bailed her out of trouble in some of the most dangerous places in the world on many occasions. Her appearance, her youthfulness, and her gender tended to make people underestimate her, but she never passed up an opportunity to prove them wrong.

His thoughts abruptly turned to the team. Pete Sabrowski was a good friend who also served with Brad in Afghanistan, and the man was one of the best pilots he knew. The guy could fly anything that could be flown and probably a few things that couldn't. He was a vital part of Brad's team on most of their missions. Like Brad, Pete was single and always ready for the next big adventure. Whether he was working with Brad or enjoying a little recreational pastime of skydiving or white water rafting, he had an unceasing thirst for action. Hunting grizzly bears in the wilds of Alaska was right up his alley.

Jared Smoot, whom he needed to go find very shortly, was another member of Force Recon Brad had served with. He had graduated with distinction at the top of his class at both the Scout Sniper basic course and the Scout Snipers Team Leader course at Marine Corps Base in Quantico, Virginia. These schools were generally considered to be the most difficult and challenging courses offered by the Corps.

Jared possessed an uncanny ability to make shots with his M40A5 well beyond its design capabilities. The rifle had started out its life as a bolt action Remington 700, but by the time the USMC armorers at Marine Corps Base Quantico were through with it, the stock rifle was no longer recognizable; it was, in fact, one of the finest sniper rifles in the world. Jared was just as at home with the legendary .50 caliber Barrett M107, and, unless Brad missed his guess, it was the Barrett that Ving would specify for this trip.

Grizzly bears could weigh up to nine hundred pounds and there were records of the animals reaching a height of over nine feet. Shooting one in full charge with the M40A5's 7.62mm NATO match round would do little more than piss off the monster unless the bullet placement was very *precise and* very lucky. The Barrett might at least slow it down enough to enable the shooter to get off a second shot. A charging grizzly bear tends to make even the iron nerves of a professional sniper a little shaky.

Charlie Dawkins, Jessica's newest boyfriend, was the unknown quantity in the equation, and Brad hated unknowns on a mission. In truth, the unknown was only the second factor in his instinctive mistrust of the man. The first factor was that Brad was really uncomfortable with the idea of anyone sleeping with his cousin. It wasn't jealousy or anything like that, just that she had always been his "little" cousin and he was probably overprotective of her. Even if his dislike of the man was partly personal, unknown factors increased the risks to his men.

Brad recognized that Pete was a good judge of character. If Charlie had become good friends with Pete, that was a little reassuring, but there was still something off about the guy. Brad felt anxious to get a full background on him before they reached their destination. He wasn't sure there was anything at all wrong with the man, but he felt absolutely convinced of one thing: Charlie

Dawkins was hiding something, and that, Brad decided, wasn't good.

Where the hell did Charlie come from? Jessica had been pretty vague about his background. The only thing she would say was that she'd met him at her father's country club. Had Jack introduced them? Wondering whether Jack had introduced the couple sent Brad's mind into a few places he really didn't want to go. Jack had been good to Brad and his mother after Brad's father died. But, he wasn't the most honest person Brad had ever met.

Brad drained his coffee and stood up, stretching and yawning. He was tired, but he could sleep on the plane. Glancing at his watch, he figured he had saved just enough time to run by Jared's house and wake him up. He knew the man had been fighting insomnia since their return from Africa, a side effect of the medications and antibiotics the doctors had given him for the bullet wound he'd suffered in the Central African Republic.

The fact that Jared had gotten river water in the wound while helping Brad rescue Jessica from a band of blood diamond-trafficking rebels had sent the docs into near apoplexy when they got back, and they loaded his system up with the latest drugs. Jared was fully recovered from his wound, but he was still experiencing complications from the meds. More than likely he was fast asleep and hadn't heard the phone or his beeper. The man slept hard when he finally managed to get some sleep.

Brad bent over and shook Jessica awake. "Time to go, sunshine," he said with a smile as she uncovered her sleepy face. *If that bastard Charlie did anything to hurt her, he'd pay. He'd pay big time.*

JARED

Brad parked his pickup in Jared's driveway and looked at Jessica. She had been anxious and agitated since learning Charlie's plane was missing. She didn't know which was worse. If it flew off the radar or landed somewhere where there was no contact. She was quiet and stared out the window as he loaded her gear in the bed of the big four-door pickup truck. He climbed out of the cab and walked quickly up to the door of Jared's three-bedroom ranch house. The lights were on in the living room, so he only knocked once before opening the door and going inside.

Jared was asleep on the sofa. A half-empty cup of hot chocolate sat on the coffee table beside him and his left arm was hanging off the couch, dangling down to the carpet.

Brad grinned. Jared's near fetish for hot cocoa was legendary among his friends. The big, rangy Texan managed to carry what he called his "makin's" wherever he went, and he drank hot cocoa before he settled down to sleep no matter how damned hard it was to prepare it. Brad had watched him scoop a hole in the desert floor near Fallujah to make his drink, under the very eyes of Taliban troops they were surveilling on a long-range reconnaissance.

Jared had dug deep into the sand behind a shallow dune and made a stove out of a tin can, perforating top and bottom with the tip of his custom knife. He placed a heat tab inside the can and carefully struck a match from one of his MRE accessory packs to the blue tablet, ensuring that any possible light from the flame would not be visible to the people they were watching.

He had judiciously measured a quantity of water into his canteen cup, and then he removed the clear plastic bag of his "makin's" from his rucksack and meticulously added just the exact amount of the powdery substance into the water, stirring it with a plastic spoon. He had explained to Brad a thousand times that the mixture had to be stirred in after the cup was placed on the flames but before the water began to heat. Then he slowly stirred the drink until steam began to rise from the cup, which *had* to be removed from the flames before the cocoa began to boil. Nothing short of an assault by the Taliban would have made the man deviate from his ritual. Brad had only seen that happen once, and Jared's wrath had been an awesome thing to behold.

"Wake up, brother," he said, gently shaking the Texan's shoulder. Noise hadn't wakened him, but Brad's touch tore him from sleep instantly.

Jared looked confused as he sat up, and then he glanced down at the watch on his wrist. "Jesus Christ, Brad, I just now finally got to sleep!"

"You've been out at least three hours, my brother," Brad said with a grin as he pointed to Jared's cell phone. "You've got two voicemails from Ving on your phone and your beeper is going off in your bedroom."

Jared cocked his head, and he could faintly hear the sound of his beeper coming from the master bedroom. "Shit!" he said, getting up and stumbling to his bedroom to grab the device.

"What's so important you had to wake me up this early in the morning?" he asked as he came back into the living room in his stocking feet.

"Pete's plane went down somewhere around Stephan Lake Lodge above Talkeetna. We're going to go find him and bring him home," Brad said soberly.

Jared was instantly wide awake, putting on his boots and going to his closet for his "D" bag. "What are you waiting for?" he called out as he opened the gun safe in his closet. His hand came out with a web belt and holster with the .45 in it, which he tossed over his shoulder. He reached back inside for his M40A5, but Brad stayed his hand.

"You're going to need the Barrett," he said. "Remember? The grizzlies?"

"Shit! I hope we don't run into one of those bastards up there. They're mean as hell and hard to kill." He lifted the big Barrett out of the safe and put it in a hard-shell case along with the .45. He reached for a second case, much smaller, and added half a box of .45 ammo and a dozen rounds for the Barrett. "We got ammo resupply up there?"

Brad nodded. "Hank's got it all set up."

"Good," Jared said, shouldering his bag and carrying the hard-shell case as if it were empty. "Time's a wastin'. Let's get this show on the road!" He strode out the door, leaving it to Brad to close and lock the front door.

Jared set the gun case and his bag into the back of the truck beside Brad's and Jessica's. "What's up with that?" he asked, jerking a thumb in Jessica's direction as he opened the back door of the truck and climbed in.

"*That,*" Jessica said, rolling her eyes, "is me going to Alaska with you."

"Jesus, girl, do you know how freakin' cold it gets up there?"

"Yes Jared," Jessica replied, mildly sarcastic. She liked the big Texan, but his overprotectiveness galled her.

"Charlie's with Pete, Jared," Brad said.

"Oh shit, I forgot about that!"

"She would have gone whether we took her or not. I figured it's better if I'm able to keep an eye on her."

"Hey guys," Jessica yelled, "I'm sitting right here, I can hear every word you're saying!"

The two men laughed, knowing she was irate and knowing just as well that she'd get over it quickly.

"I didn't mean anything by it," Brad said, grinning.

"Shut up and drive," Jessica muttered. But she was grinning too.

JESSICA AND CHARLIE

Jessica was concerned for Charlie's safety, and Pete's as well, because he was a good friend. She adored all her cousin's friends and they felt the same about her. Charlie was different though. Charlie made her heart beat hard in her chest. He was handsome, intelligent, mysterious, and there was a bad boy quality to him that made him irresistible.

She had met him at her father's country club, some kind of political thing that Jack Paul wanted her to attend. She hadn't really wanted to go, but he'd been insistent and she had finally given in. Jack

Paul was rich, vain, and self-centered, but he *was* her father and he *did* give her money every month. The money, combined with what she earned with the principal of her trust fund, enabled her to do the research so necessary to continue doing what she loved so much. Jessica was a treasure hunter, and a moderately successful one at that.

In the past six years she actually made money in her hunt for treasure, though she had wisely invested most of it, something neither her father nor her cousin Brad knew. It wouldn't be long before she could tell her father that she didn't need his monthly check anymore, and she was looking forward to that day. Maybe then Jack would take her a little more seriously.

The last few months she had been researching a story she uncovered of a lost gold mine in Alaska. The story had been recorded in a handwritten journal she picked up at, oddly enough, a garage sale in Dallas. The seller, an older woman who had just moved to the Dallas-Fort Worth area from Seattle, let the musty old journal go for five dollars, but only after regaling her with a tale of her great-grandfather's disappearance shortly after he sent word to his family that he had struck the mother lode. Apparently, he disappeared before he ever managed to return home and had never been heard from again.

Jessica had been surprised that the woman would let such a keepsake go, but the woman confessed that she was glad to be rid of it. "I could tell you stories that would curl your hair," the woman had said with a bitter, distant stare in her eyes. "I've lost uncles and cousins who couldn't resist the lure of that legend. It's a curse on my family and I'll be glad to be rid of it." Jessica had been transfixed, and she had gladly paid the money.

She shivered deliciously. Charlie took her seriously. He was genuinely interested in her work, and he seemed to really enjoy helping her in her research. After Jack had introduced them at the club, Charlie had politely asked what she did for a living over a pair of mint juleps that she barely tasted. He was so good looking and he seemed very interested in her.

When she first told him what she did, he didn't seem interested. She had nearly come to the conclusion that he was showing polite interest only because he had designs on her body, and for once that didn't truly offend her. She had no objections to an occasional tumble with the right man. It was when she mentioned the lost mine near Mount Watana that he had perked up and started to show a sincere curiosity in her work.

After the drinks they had made their exit from the gathering, Jack having long since disappeared into one of the club rooms. He liked to smoke smuggled Cuban cigars and drink from the very expensive bottle of fifty-year-old Macallan single malt scotch the club kept for him.

Charlie had driven her home, asking questions about her research into the old mine legend, and when she invited him in to see the journal, he had happily agreed. The evening seemed to stretch on forever, and, by sunrise, Charlie had joined the very select and extremely small group of men who had been privileged to share her bed.

What she thought of as a once-in-a-lifetime lark turned into something more, and they had since spent a good deal of time with their heads together, poring over her research. He had never honestly come right out and told her what he did for a living, he had just hinted at being on sabbatical. His interest in her work somewhat gave her the impression that he might be a college professor or an archaeologist, and in truth he reminded her of her favorite movie character, Indiana Jones. Charlie even looked a little like the actor who had played the character.

She had introduced him to Pete, and Pete had taken a real shine to him right away. When the three of them got to talking about Alaska and Pete had mentioned going grizzly hunting at Stephan Lake Lodge, Charlie had been fascinated, and before Jessica knew it, Pete had invited him along on his hunting trip. She'd had no desire to kill a grizzly, and she'd demurred when they'd asked her along even though her latest treasure hunt would eventually take her there. There was a lot more she wanted to know and much more extensive research to be done before she would make the trip up to the last frontier.

She wasn't *really* worried about Charlie. Pete was an incredibly resourceful man and she knew he was an expert at cold weather survival, but if either of them were truly hurt, she wanted to be there for them.

CHAPTER FIVE

LEWIS HOSTBACK

Day 2 0630 hours AKDT

Lewis awakened early in the morning, as was his habit. His personal routine never varied. Up at 0430, he did an hour of calisthenics, and then he either ran or skied, depending on the weather, for two miles at the fastest pace he could manage under the circumstances. He followed his exercise routine with a half hour in his personal wood-fired sauna, hand-built from a diagram out of a Finnish Army manual. He followed this by rolling naked in the snow, or, in the late spring and summer, a quick dip in the frigid snowmelt waters of the stream at the bottom of the hill behind his hut.

The low flying Piper that had passed directly over their compound the night before troubled him. The fact that it crashed just afterwards provided no consolation. He knew that if whoever was in that plane survived, they might have gotten an up-close-and-personal look at their mining operation. Familiar enough with the area, he realized if there were survivors they would be unable to communicate with anyone from the outside. For that, he was thankful. That would buy him some time before any intruders would be able to share news of their potential discovery.

The very first item the Order of Phineas had purchased with their initial gold nuggets was an extraordinarily expensive piece of electronic equipment that the salesman had assured him would jam any frequencies used by cell phones, radios, satellite phones, or any other commonly available communications equipment. There was even an adjustment that allowed him to unblock a certain bandwidth for the Order's private use and then close it up again when they no longer needed it. It had been incredibly expensive to buy and transport to their base camp, and the building that housed it was costly to build as well.

Any survivors, however, would be eager to tell anyone who came to rescue them about what they might have seen, and that was not something he was prepared to live with.

Lewis Hostback was an arrogant man, a supreme egotist. He had been chosen by the people of this Aryan Nations splinter group as their leader, but he was ill-equipped for the role. The only things he truly brought to the Order aside from his obvious physical prowess were his charisma and his determination.

Lewis was an imposing figure of a man, well over six feet tall and possessing the massive chest, shoulders, and arms of an old-time lumberjack. In fact, he had played inside linebacker for part of a season with the Packers in Green Bay until he permitted his personal prejudices to alienate him from his non-white teammates. Despite his superior abilities on the field, he had been ostracized for his comments, his contract terminated.

A sympathetic friend convinced him to move to Coeur d'Alene, Idaho, where he'd used the generous severance package the team had paid him to abrogate his contract to buy a cabin on the lake in a wooded region outside the town. His friend introduced him to the Aryan Brotherhood, and he had been welcomed with open arms for what they considered to be his "stand for the superiority and purity of the white race."

His progress up through the ranks had been meteoric. The Brotherhood needed all the favorable press it could get, and Lewis Hostback represented a poster-boy "Mr. Clean". He didn't drink, smoke or even swear, and he never missed a Sunday sermon in church. He also possessed a deep bass voice that made him a welcome addition to church choirs wherever he went.

What the Brotherhood did not know was that he maintained the "Mr. Clean" façade to cover a violent temper and dangerous psychotic tendencies, tendencies that often exploded into intensely violent acts that he was very careful to cover up. He never left a witness to one of his explosions . . . at least he'd never left a *living* witness.

When August B. Kreis III had stepped down from the leadership of the Tabernacle of the Phineas Priesthood-Aryan Nations, the whole of Aryan Nations had been thrown into turmoil. The members of the Coeur d'Alene chapter rebelled and separated from the splinter group and selected Hostback as their spiritual leader.

Hostback named their group The Order of Phineas. Phineas was a character in the Book of Hebrews who slew an Israelite man and a Midianite woman while they engaged in intercourse in the man's tent, running a javelin through the man's back and the belly of the woman. The Bible story is often used by white supremacist groups to justify acts of cruel violence against people who practice miscegenation—the mixing of two races.

The Order had been run out of Coeur d'Alene two years before, and Hostback led his followers to sanctuary in the Nelchina Public Use Area. He had heard legends of riches in gold being found in the region, and he convinced his followers they were entitled to live on public land. After all, they were citizens, and the ZOG maintained no right to deny them access to land owned by citizens. He paid for most of the migration out of his own pocket.

Hostback thought that Nelchina would be perfect for them for a number of reasons. Its immense size and low population density was the most obvious attraction. There were damned few neighbors in Alaska once you got outside the main cities, and what neighbors there were tended to mind their own business. The Nelchina Public Use Area was even better. There were *no* neighbors because the government didn't permit anyone to build there.

Another reason Nelchina seemed perfect was that the people in Alaska *loved* guns, *depended* on them. Going around armed seemed as natural as breathing. Nelchina, Alaska was a perfect fit for Lewis Hostback and the Order of Phineas.

Now, just as their placer mining operations were beginning to produce some real money, they were in danger of exposure. Lewis knew that he was being paranoid, but he felt certain that when the red Piper had buzzed over their compound it had to have been on some kind of reconnaissance mission for the ZOG. He truly believed that if there were in fact survivors of the crash, it was only a matter of time until the Feds came after them.

He was determined to keep their sanctuary a secret from the outside world and was prepared to do whatever it took to ensure that the secret remained unbroken. If it was necessary to hunt down and kill the interlopers then that was just too bad for them. *My will be done.* The unconscious blasphemy didn't register with him. Lewis Hostback was a bona fide psychopath.

CRASH SITE

They came across the wreckage late in the afternoon, approximately twenty miles from their base camp. Lewis, as usual, insisted on using cross-country skis to hunt for the site. The noise of snowmobiles would echo through the valleys and mountains, and sound carried a long way in the frigid air. There was no need to draw attention to themselves from the rare hunter or trapper in the deserted territory. Motorized vehicles were forbidden and therefore objects of curiosity. Hostback led a team of a dozen armed men spread out in a line, each just far enough apart to maintain visual contact with the next man.

Hostback had seen the smoke rising from a fire not far from the wreckage and called in his team using hand signals so that the survivors wouldn't be alerted to their presence. Lewis lay in the snow and eyed the crash site with an objective eye through a pair of excellent high-powered Zeiss binoculars.

The Piper had come down at the bottom of the south slope of Mount Watana, almost reaching the surface of the narrow river at its foot. From what Lewis could see, the plane had failed to clear the last of the tall, narrow firs and had lost a wing before coming down hard on its side and sliding for several hundred feet. He winced. That had to have hurt. There was a body covered with a silver thermal blanket next to the shattered and burned fuselage.

It looked as if the survivors, two men whose features were impossible to make out due to their arctic clothing, had dragged the body back over the ice to the fuselage after the fire burned out. The survivors built a sort of reflector wall of green logs to build their fire behind, just up the bank from the ice, and they huddled behind it. Whoever they were, their fieldcraft was impressive.

"Get as close as you can before opening up on them. If they think we're a rescue party it should be easy enough to eliminate them." If anyone in the hunter team had an objection to killing the interlopers, they kept it to themselves. Lewis Hostback was the leader, the pastor of their Order, and his word was law.

As with any military type mission, anything that can possibly go wrong will go wrong; soldiers are quite familiar with Murphy's Law. Everett Samples, at sixteen the youngest member of the Order of Phineas, became overexcited when one of the survivors stood up with a rifle in his hands. He quickly lifted his M-16, which was slung across his chest the way he had seen the soldiers and SWAT team guys on TV do it before they had left the lower forty-eight, and let loose a long burst from the rifle.

It only takes one point seven seconds to empty an M-16's thirty-round magazine, and Everett sprayed most of his magazine into the air above the survivors' heads. His first round struck the wooden heat reflector, but muzzle hop had thrown the rest of the burst high.

The standing survivor reacted immediately, throwing himself to the ground behind the logs. The one who hadn't stood up aimed carefully from behind the logs and shot Everett center mass, dropping him like a sack of grain. The other members of the Order had begun firing furiously as soon as Everett had screwed up, and Lewis frantically signaled them to break into two teams and flank the survivors as he had trained them.

Two more members of the Order fell before the two teams arranged themselves and began to advance on the defensive position by fire and maneuver.

PETE AND CHARLIE

"I'll be damned!" Charlie shouted, standing up. "Here comes the cavalry!"

Pete glanced in the direction Charlie was staring just in time to see one of the advancing party lift the muzzle of an M-16 slung around his neck and open up on them. Instinctively, he dove for his M-14 and rolled into a kneeling position behind the reflector they'd built to keep themselves warm and returned fire. The guy firing the M-16 full auto went down, but by then the whole damned group was shooting at them.

"Grab whatever you can and let's get the hell outta here!" he roared, frantically stuffing his feet into the bindings of his newfangled snowshoes. He had no idea who the hell these trigger-happy maniacs were and no intention of sticking around to find out. These guys looked serious! Pete glanced over the reflector once more and noticed that the group had separated into two fire teams.

They were doing a pretty damned reasonable facsimile of fire and maneuver, a military tactic where one team laid down covering fire while the other team rushed a few yards and fell down into prone firing positions so they could in turn provide covering fire for the other team to advance. It looked pretty well practiced to him. "Run!" he screamed at Charlie.

* * *

Lewis was furious with his men for screwing up what should have been an easy capture, but the kid who screwed it up had already paid the ultimate price for his impatience. Lewis poked through the wreckage and around the still burning fire, but there was little there except for the dead body. He ordered his men onwards. "These guys aren't amateurs," he shouted, convinced more than ever that the survivors were from the ZOG, sent to spy on the Order of Phineas.

"Watch what you're doing and remember your training." He didn't waste any more breath. Lewis knew that their very survival was dependent on keeping their existence a secret from the outside world.

Pete and Charlie ran as if all the hounds of hell were after them. They had a halfway decent head start, and they couldn't see any sign of the pursuit. From time to time Pete raised his hand for them to halt so that he could listen, and usually he could hear a few sounds of their pursuers. The snow was deep and the going unbelievably rugged, but Charlie seemed no more winded than Pete. Pete's respect for the younger man went up a notch. There was more to the kid than he'd suspected.

Pete looked up at the sky and saw that the weather appeared to be worsening and darkness would come early. Both those facts gave him a tactical advantage over their pursuers, and he fully intended to take advantage of them. He patted the claymore bag strapped to his side. He needed to put a little more distance between himself and Charlie and their pursuers, but, as soon as he did, Pete was certain he'd be able to even the odds up a bit. Whoever these fruitcakes might be, they were about to discover that fucking with one of Uncle Sam's Misguided Children was a damned serious tactical error—a fatal one.

What the fuck is wrong with them? Why the fuck are they trying to kill us? Pete kept too busy moving to articulate his thoughts. Charlie was keeping up and showing no signs of flagging. He didn't even seem surprised. *Does this kid know something I don't?*

CHAPTER SIX

TALKEETNA

Day 2 1500 hours AKDT

"Talkeetna. Where the road ends and life begins."

Talkeetna, Alaska can be found at the convergence of three rivers, the Susitna, Chulitna and Talkeetna. In 2010, the U.S. census measured the population at a little under nine hundred souls. The local economy is based principally on tourism and the associated activities of flightseeing, rafting, mountain biking, hiking, camping, fishing and hunting. Approximately midway between Anchorage and the entrance to Denali National Park, the population of the little town grows enormously from April through July as mountain climbers assemble to prepare to scale Mount McKinley.

It had taken a good deal of arguing and a hefty bonus to get the pilot of the DeHavilland Beaver to make the flight to Talkeetna from Anchorage because the weather situation was still dicey. The man only agreed to take the flight after Brad explained the circumstances to him, and even then he only took them because his brother was a Marine Lance Corporal at Camp Pendleton. The Corps family is large and it sticks together.

All of them visibly relaxed when the aircraft settled to the earth of the primitive airfield in Talkeetna with a firm thump after skittering sideways on its final approach. It had been a rough one-hundred-odd-mile flight.

Brad intended to utilize their time as efficiently as possible. He was fully aware that in a survival situation, every minute counted. He had no intention of leaving Pete and Charlie exposed any longer than absolutely necessary. When he exited the plane, his mind had already shifted into what he thought of, for lack of a better description, as combat mode.

He motioned for Jared to stick with the pilot and see to the offloading of their luggage and gear. Then he waved Tom over to the Tamsco hangar where he spotted a pristine Bell 212 Twin painted a startling red with brilliant white trim. "That's the only chopper I see, Tom; check and verify that's the one Hank's laid on for us." Tom set out at a brisk pace, almost a jog, toward the open hangar door. A small motorized luggage cart chugged toward the Beaver. Brad, Ving, and Jessica walked toward the Quonset hut that served as a terminal at the tiny airport.

"The troopers have an office inside the terminal," Ving said. "We're supposed to meet Lieutenant Ben Robinson in there; he's the guy in charge of the search and rescue op."

"How many men do they have on this operation?" Brad asked.

"I couldn't get a straight answer to that question on the phone." Ving sounded aggravated, but Brad wondered if it might just have been the man's reaction to the rough flight.

Brad grunted. "Did Hank say he had everything set for us up here?"

Ving had called the logistics expert when they'd landed in Anchorage.

"Yeah, he said the chopper's confirmed and the package David Henderson sent from Fort Greeley had been picked up by the troopers. He said it was a crate and that Lieutenant Robinson already signed for it. The ammo's in the crate with the rest of the gear." Brad nodded, continuing his walk to the Quonset hut with Jessica and Ving trailing him.

The Quonset hut was nothing more than several semicircular sections of corrugated galvanized steel assembled in a series. From outside it looked like the top half of a large piece of pipe just lying on the ground with a door and a window on one end of it. Brad was a bit surprised that the terminal was so small.

As they entered the front door, Brad felt a blast of heat hit him in the face. There were only two people inside that he could see. One, apparently an airline employee, was working at a makeshift ticket counter. The other, in the blue two-tone uniform of the Alaska State Troopers, remained seated in a swivel chair at a desk near the back of the building under an Alaska State Troopers emblem on the wall.

Brad was a little taken aback. He had been expecting to see some kind of command center with at least three or four troopers coordinating the search operation. Ving had told him how short-handed Robinson was, but he'd expected the man would call in reinforcements for an emergency. Apparently things were significantly different here than in the lower forty-eight.

Brad, Ving and Jessica approached the trooper who was staring at them with frank interest; he looked to be paying particular attention to Jessica.

Brad approached the large man and held out his hand. "I'm Brad Jacobs," he said. The lieutenant unleashed a hell of a strong grip. "This is my cousin, Jessica Paul and I do believe you spoke to Mason Ving on the phone."

Robinson released Brad's hand but did not make an effort to shake Ving or Jessica's hands. "Ben Robinson. I'm surprised you got that guy to fly up here in this weather. I expected you would be stuck in Anchorage until the weather let up some." He glanced out the window at the darkening sky. "Whenever that may be."

Jessica went to the window and stared out for a long time. Then she turned her attention to bulletins and announcements pinned to a corkboard. She wondered how many small planes went down in the Alaskan wilderness and how many of them were never recovered.

Brad made a non-committal gesture with his free hand. "We don't stand down because of weather conditions."

Robinson gave him a hard look. "I checked on you after your man Ving there called me. You've got a reputation as a hard ass in the Corps, and Henderson up at Fort Greeley says you did really well at N.W.T.C."

The big trooper put his hands on his hips. "Except for my time in the Corps, I've lived up here all my life. I've hunted, fished, and trapped this country since I was old enough to strap on a pair of skis. Since I got back from the big sandbox, I've had to read a page from the Good Book to some pretty hard men that made the Taliban look like Boy Scouts.

"I've also hauled the remains of some hardheads who wouldn't listen to reason out of the backcountry on an ahkio, too. I don't want to have to do that with your friends and I don't want to do that with you either."

Brad knew he was antagonizing the only real help available in the frozen northland, but his stubborn pride wouldn't permit him to acknowledge it.

"Can you give me an update on the rescue mission status?"

Robinson's eyes turned stone cold. "Until this blackbird storm lets up, there's not much I can tell you. From what I've seen of the latest satellite imagery from N.O.A.A (the National Oceanic and Atmospheric Administration operates a public access website publishing the latest satellite imagery, updated every few hours), when this one lets up, we're going to have no more than a twenty-four hour window before the next one hits. I'll have eyes in the air the minute it's safe to fly."

"That's all?" Brad was unable to keep the irritation out of his voice.

"Easy Brad," Ving said, touching his friend on the shoulder, trying to calm him down.

"I don't believe this!" Brad exclaimed, shaking Ving's hand off and giving the big trooper a hard look.

"Let me explain a few things to you, Tex. Alaska is like another country, maybe even a whole other world from the one you live in. We have damned little government or regulation and no budget to speak of. I've only got three other troopers to patrol an area of over twenty-five thousand square miles of the most rugged terrain in the world. Most of our patrolling has to be done by dog sled teams or by helicopter.

"Motorized vehicles including snow mobiles are prohibited in most of the wilderness areas except for emergencies or special projects because it's just too dangerous to try to operate them in this kind of terrain. We have an Arctic Cat, but I have to get permission from the trooper commander down in Fairbanks before I'm allowed to take it out into the back country.

"This part of Alaska is known as no man's land. In the areas around the perimeter of Anchorage we have plenty of resources, but out here we have to rely primarily on air search by cooperative bush pilots and volunteer groups.

"Down here in Talkeetna the weather might be acceptable for flying, but we're at three hundred feet elevation. Up around Mount Watana, where we initially picked up your friends' ELT signal, it's over six thousand feet. They've got blizzard conditions and the weather is much worse than it is here. There's no way I can get air search moving up there until the weather clears."

"How many were on board the aircraft?" Brad asked. He knew the man was telling the truth, but frustration began building inside him. He felt like a pressure cooker about to explode.

"Just your two guys and the pilot . . . a good man, Sam Henderson."

"We're gonna go now," Brad said firmly, looking to Ving who nodded in agreement.

"You'll go by yourselves, provided you can get Tamsco to fly in this crap. It's let up a little, but, like I said, my nose tells me you've got twenty-four hours, probably much less, before you get socked in again. I'd advise against it."

Brad faced Ving, whose face showed no emotion at all. "Check with Tom and see if our charter pilot is ready to go. If he won't fly tell Tom to get familiar with the chopper. While you're at it, make sure the ammo Henderson sent is correct and onboard."

"On it," Ving said tightly. He didn't like it, but he wasn't about to upbraid Brad at this point. His friend was wrapped as tight as Ving had ever seen him and pissing him off would serve no good purpose. Ving was straight up New Orleans born and bred, and even though he'd passed the N.W.T.C. course he hated Alaska and the cold. The only reason he'd come on this mission was his loyalty to Brad and Pete. Ving let himself out of the building and realized the temperature had dropped in the few minutes they'd been inside the building.

"You guys are crazy," Robinson exclaimed. "If you guys go up there you're on your own. Hell, I don't need two groups of people to find and rescue."

"Don't worry," Brad replied. "I don't plan on getting lost."

Robinson seemed as if he had something else to say, but he bit it back and sat back down in his desk chair, fuming.

Brad realized the man was right, but he also knew some things that Robinson did not. He and his team were expert trackers and survivalists, trained and experienced in extreme cold weather operations. Despite Robinson's assertions about the harshness of the Alaskan wilderness, Brad and his men had fought and survived in the wild and rugged mountains of Nuristan Province in Afghanistan. The team thrived in hostile environments where most men couldn't survive and it was Holy Writ that they never left a man behind.

"Show me on this map exactly where you picked up the ELT signal," Brad said, unfolding an acetate-covered U.S. military topographical map and spreading it on top of Robinson's desk.

"That's another part of the problem you aren't taking into consideration," the now surly Trooper said. "I can give you the exact coordinates of the signal we received, but I can't be certain that the coordinates are accurate. We received only a short, intermittent signal from their ELT after they dropped off local radar. Radar works 'line of sight'. As soon as they dropped lower than the mountaintops, radar lost contact with them. I have no way of knowing how far they glided after we lost contact; all I can give you is their last known location and their flight bearing."

"But the ELT should still be transmitting...."

"The ELT may have been damaged on impact. These small plane ELTs are not as powerful as the big ones they use in commercial airliners. And there's still the problem of the mountains blocking the signals. The ELT might be working just fine, but you'll never receive the signal until there's nothing between you but air. That's a common problem up here and we deal with it every day."

"No radio contact?" Brad asked.

"Same problem."

"Just what type of support can I count on from you?" Brad asked. He was exasperated and reaching the ragged edge limits of his patience. He was tired of being nice and wanted answers.

"I don't have any troopers to put on the ground. Air search is ready to go as soon as the weather clears on the mountain. I've also alerted our two best volunteer groups to assist with the ground search and they are mobilizing as we speak. They can leave as soon as we get a break in the weather. The Alaska Mountain Rescue Group (AMRG) and the Alaska Search and Rescue Association (ASARA) should both have support up here in the next few hours, but neither of them is going to send men up there before the weather clears."

"That's the best you can do?" Brad asked.

"Don't underestimate the capabilities of these organizations, Jacobs. They're both extremely effective at this type of search and rescue operation. They work with us on dozens of searches every year."

"What's the nearest town or village to the last ELT coordinates you got?"

"You're standing in it," the trooper replied evenly, his own temper fraying. "Talkeetna is the only real town for hundreds of miles. If your friends are able to hike out, the closest place with a small airstrip and year-round basic facilities is their original destination, the hunting lodge on Stephan Lake. It's roughly twenty miles of god awful rugged terrain from the area we think they went down to the lodge."

"Any local residents living anywhere in the vicinity we might be able to contact if we need to?"

Ben Robinson started to open his mouth, but it snapped shut quickly. "None that I can recommend." His eyes told Brad it would be useless to press him further on the subject.

That seemed like an odd response to Brad, but his intuition told him he was wasting his time.

"We're going anyway," Brad said shortly. "We'll maintain radio contact or call on the satellite phone every hour with an update on our status, at least as long as we can maintain satellite service. I don't imagine the mountains will interfere with that." Disgusted, he turned and headed out the front door toward the Tamsco hangar followed by Jessica.

ROBINSON

Ben Robinson leaned the back of his chair toward the wall and raised his hands, clasping them behind his head. *No, the mountains won't screw up your satellite transmissions, but mountains ain't the only problems you're going to run into, Tex. You may not be a* cheechako, *but you ain't ready for what I'm afraid those mountains are hiding. This country isn't kind to tenderfoots.*

Now I can't say for sure, but the old timers and the poachers and the illegal prospectors talk when they get liquored up down at the Trading Post, and I'm hearing some ugly rumors that I hope to God ain't true.

They're saying there's a passel of men out there in the valley, armed men, men that don't like anybody poking around in their business. Amos Flagg, that old degenerate, says a bunch of the old poachers have come up missing. He's hinted that they ain't ever coming back and that Old Man Winter didn't get them, these men did.

I haven't found any proof, but I'm afraid old Amos is right. The Air Force says they've had instances where their communications were jammed, and that takes some serious electronic equipment and knowhow. I wish they could have pinpointed it, but they couldn't. Yep, there's something going on up the valley, but I don't have the time or the resources to take care of the responsibilities I already have. I didn't have the heart to tell old Tex that there are three other groups of hunters that have been reported missing, and I've got to hunt all three of them.

Fortunately for Tex, none of those other groups have the training, the experience or the equipment that he has. I can keep an ear open for his "updates", but I'm afraid that, Marine or not, Tex is going to be pretty much on his own. I hope he's as good as he thinks he is. That was one fine looking woman he had with him. Wish she were going to be keeping me warm tonight!

Ben smiled ruefully. He lived at home with his mother, a full blood Inuit. He had taken her in when his father died, and she would raise holy hell if he brought home a fancy blonde from the lower forty-eight.

CHAPTER SEVEN

GREEN LIGHT

There was a crate beside the chopper bearing a stencil identifying it as property of the U.S. Government with the return address of the N.W.T.C. Annex at Black Rapids. As Ving approached the chopper, he could see the pilot performing a preflight check.

"Your partner is in the office, taking care of the paperwork," the pilot called out without taking his eyes off the bird. He heard voices and looked up. "Correction. He's coming out now with some blonde girl. Surely you're not taking her with you."

Ving answered the man's question with his own question. "Are we ready to go?" Ving asked smiling, though he wasn't happy about this mission. There was a bad feeling in the pit of his stomach, something he ordinarily paid a great deal of attention to. Ben Robinson had been so friendly on the phone after he'd identified himself and Brad as former members of Force Recon, but there was something definitely off-kilter about the man in person. He wished Brad hadn't gotten off on the wrong foot with the big lieutenant. Ving was willing to bet there were important facts the man was not telling them.

Shit! It was bad enough Mama Ving's little boy Mason had to be running around in the ice and snow freezing his ass off looking for Pete; nope, the big state trooper, a half-assed Eskimo himself by the looks of him, had to go piling mystery on top of it all. Ving shook his head. He had to do this; Pete was in trouble. In the end, that was all that mattered. *Semper Fi!*

"I doubt it," the pilot said laconically. "Weather's still dicey and it doesn't appear as if it's getting better anytime soon. Even if we get a break it ain't likely to last."

"Come on, man, I know Hank told you guys this was an emergency. We've got friends down out there!"

"You can't help 'em none if we get ourselves killed tryin' to get there!"

"I know damned well this bird can fly in this crap! I've ridden through worse than this...."

"In a 212 Twin?" the pilot asked skeptically.

"A UH-1N, and that's the same damned thing!"

The pilot's eyes clouded over. "Where'd you ride a UH-1N?" he asked quietly.

"Nuristan Province, Afghanistan," Ving answered evenly. "They had to use the UH-1N for the altitude. We needed to get up around seventeen thousand feet with a full load to take it to the Taliban."

"Army?"

"Force Recon."

The pilot worked his jaws almost as if he were chewing tobacco for a minute, and Ving could practically see the wheels spinning in the man's head.

"Fuck it; load your shit up, brother. Never let it be said that Harvey Messer let down the Marines, but I'm tellin' you now, if the weather takes a turn for the worse, I'm hightailin' my ass right back here. I ain't no hero." The man stepped forward and they shook hands. Ving walked over to the crate and started prying off the top. Messer helped.

They had the *ahkio* out and on the ground beside the chopper by the time Jared arrived riding on the baggage cart with their gear. Tom walked out of the office a moment later. The four of them got it all unloaded by the time Brad and Jessica walked into the hangar.

Ving motioned Brad to one side for a quiet conference, and Jessica went straight to the weapons cases, lifting out the one Ving had marked with her name. As Ving explained the pilot's reluctant acceptance of the charter to Brad, he kept an eye on the slender young blonde. She looked comfortable with the odd looking M4A1, her nimble fingers skimming gracefully over the weapon checking for dust or damage. Her movements were swift and sure, and when she inserted the loaded magazine in the well and tapped the bottom with the heel of her hand to ensure it was seated, she did it with the confidence and skill of an expert. It would be easy to mistake her for an empty-headed swimsuit model because of her appearance, but Ving knew her to be an expert marksman and a cool head in tight situations. She was one of the most positive, confident people he had ever known, a trait she inherited from her father, Jack.

Nevertheless, he knew the treacherous country they were about to venture into, and he realized the dangers that lurked there. He would have to keep an eye on the young adventuress.

Ving's focus returned to the conversation he was having with Brad. "What's that?" he asked. "My mind was wandering, Brad, and I didn't catch that."

Brad grimaced. He had seen Ving watching Jessica and his temper had gotten the better of him. "I said something's going on up here and I don't like the smell of it. That trooper may be a Marine, and I don't think he's lying to us, but I'm pretty damned sure he's leaving something out, something important, something he doesn't want us to know."

"I'm getting the same vibe from this pilot, Brad."

Brad shook his head. "I've got a bad feeling about this, buddy, but I'm not going to let it stop me from doing my damnedest to save Pete and Charlie. Don't let the pilot notice, but make sure everyone is locked and loaded when we take off and ready for anything ... and make sure my weapon is locked and loaded too. I'm going to see if I can get anything more out of the guy at the ticket counter."

"You're not going to like this worth a damn, brother, but I wouldn't do that if I were you."

"We need more intel, Ving."

"Yeah, but you ain't gonna get it from that guy."

"So how do you propose we try to find out what we need to know, smart guy?"

"When you go fishing, brother, you got to use the right bait." Ving stared pointedly at Jessica, who was slipping into her cold weather parka and vapor barrier (VB) boots. The VB boots were essential equipment in the Arctic. There were one-way vents inside the arch in each boot to let moisture out while keeping heat in, and there were lugs for ski and snowshoe bindings built onto the heels.

Brad looked over toward the makeshift ticket counter and noticed the man ogling Jessica for all he was worth. Brad nodded his acquiescence and, while Ving went to whisper in Jessica's ear, he walked across the space to talk with the pilot. A moment later, Jessica approached the man at the ticket counter, swinging her hips and flipping her hair off her shoulders.

"What's the terrain like up there where we're headed?" Brad asked the pilot. "Robinson showed me the territory on the map...."

"I've got one," Brad said hurriedly, taking the acetate-covered map from the cargo pocket of his baggy arctic pants and laying it atop a nearby workbench. He weighted down the edges with two wrenches and a socket from the bench top and Messer pointed to the area Brad had already marked with a red grease pencil.

"Rugged is too nice a word for this region right here," Messer said, wiggling his index finger in a loose circle around the small "x". "It's a nightmare, a frozen hell up here." The contour marker showed the elevation to be nearly 5100 feet. "Depending on their altitude when the ELT started going off, they could have glided anywhere in this circle." Messer spread his fingers wide and scribed a circle roughly a mile and a half in diameter.

"That's something else I don't understand. I thought ELTs went off automatically when an aircraft impacted the ground."

Messer gave him a scornful look. "That's the way it works in the lower forty-eight, my friend. Up here, the bush pilots know the ELT signal will be shielded by the mountain peaks. As soon as they have an indication that they're in trouble, they thump the switch and set the ELT off. We'll find out for sure when we get there. If they went down so fast that the ground impact set off the ELT, there's not going to be much left of your friends." Messer's grim face told Brad that he had found wreckage from such a circumstance before.

"What about people? Are there any people or hunting cabins we can reach up there?"

Messer's face simply closed as if a curtain had been dropped across it. "Don't know nothin' about that."

Try as he might, Brad couldn't get the pilot to say another word on the subject. Irritated, he folded the map and put it in his pocket. He turned to face his team. "Saddle up! I want to get up there before dark." According to the times Robinson had given him, it shouldn't get dark until 2130 hours, but the bad weather might make it come a little earlier. The temperature was already dropping, and Jessica had come back looking dejected. Brad knew she had been unsuccessful in getting any additional information and they had no more time to waste.

OUTBOUND FROM TALKEETNA

Day 2 1530 hours AKDT

The Bell 212 Twin Huey was painted a bold red and white, which stood out against the bright green background of the forest that surrounded the airport. With the gear and team loaded, the chopper took off and headed east, following the Susitna River. It measured seventy-eight miles from the Talkeetna Airport to the coordinates Robinson had given them.

After approximately fifteen minutes Brad could see the majestic peaks of the Talkeetna Mountains poking through the top of the massive cloud layer that concealed the blackbird storm. He knew it was going to be a rough ride.

Brad put his head close to Ving's, keeping an eye on Jessica, who was sitting on the jump seat behind and between Messer and Tom, who was sitting in the co-pilot's seat.

"What did you find out on the background check?" He didn't have to mention Charlie by name; Ving knew who he was asking about.

"I called from the terminal building, Brad. He checks out clean, but there's something about it that's weird as hell."

"What's that?"

"He's got a detailed history, archaeology professor at Florida State."

"What's so weird about that?"

"His history only goes back around five years. Before that, I can't find a single mention of his existence."

"What do you make of that?" Brad knew damned well what it sounded like to *him*. It sounded like Charlie boy had been sent undercover in a hell of a hurry, and somebody in the department of obfuscation in whatever agency employed him had made a careless mistake.

"I think he's either one of the really good guys or one of the really bad guys. He knows *somebody* with good enough connections to construct a fairly solid cover identity. My guess is he's either a Fed or connected with organized crime," Ving said.

"Either way I don't like it." Brad scowled. "He's a liar. He's lied to us and he's lied to Jessica."

"If he's a Fed, he might not have a choice."

"You think he could be on a mission that involves us?"

"I'd say that's a high probability."

Brad thought about that for a second. "What in the hell would the Feds want with us?"

"Something tells me we will soon find out."

"I think it's more likely he's some kind of crook."

"That doesn't make much sense. What could he want from us?"

"I'm not sure yet. Maybe he's trying to get to Jack through Jessica. Did you find anything to connect him to Uncle Jack? That's who introduced him to Jessica."

The chopper suddenly dropped almost thirty feet and began to crab sideways against a vicious headwind. Brad had been in worse conditions than this, and he had faith in the rugged chopper. He was less certain about Messer. They were getting damned close to Mount Watana, but the weather conditions were continuing to deteriorate.

Brad glanced down at the map in his hands. The location they were headed for was way off the course between Talkeetna and Stephan Lake Lodge. What the hell had Pete and Charlie been doing way up here?

Visibility started to drop even more rapidly and high winds began buffeting the chopper as they approached their destination. Despite the poor conditions, Messer began a standard search pattern around the coordinates last received from the downed plane's ELT. The wind and the snow flurries made it difficult to see the ground. The ELT had broadcast a position that was at nearly 5100 feet in elevation toward the east side of the mountain.

Messer dropped the bird down lower to try to get a better look at the ground. That meant they were flying well below the summit of Mount Watana, and visibility had gotten so poor they could no longer see the peak. Messer was a pretty damned good chopper jockey, but Brad knew they were at serious risk of crashing into the mountainside.

Ving was starting to turn green, and Brad was beginning to understand why the Alaska State Troopers had not yet started their search. This was flying blind. He was regretting bringing Jessica along. Forget Jack's wrath if anything happened to her, Brad couldn't imagine his life without her. Especially if it were his fault. That reinforced his misgivings about Charlie. Something definitely wasn't right.

"I'm gonna give this another fifteen minutes and then I've gotta get back to Talkeetna. I'm havin' a helluva time keepin' her in the air," Messer announced to his passengers.

Brad had no intentions of giving up; they were too damned close. He could see bits and pieces of the mountain through the snow and fog. He really wanted a visual confirmation of the crash site before putting his team on the ground, but time was running out on them. Going back to Talkeetna empty-handed was not an option.

He made a command decision. "Put us down here!"

"What the fuck?" Messer screeched.

"Right fucking here, right fucking now," Brad repeated.

There was a small hole in the clouds where they could see a fairly level area on the side of the mountain that was larger than the thirty-five meters required to set the chopper down. It was just about the right altitude within about a quarter mile of the intermittent signal that had last been broadcast.

"Are you sure, man?" Messer asked.

"If you can do it without bending the bird, set us down here. We can handle the rest," Brad responded.

"I can do it, but it's going to be a touch and go insertion. I don't dare set her down, and you're going to have to offload the way you did in combat. This wind catches my bird just right and we're all dead. I'm only gonna be able to hold a hover for a couple of seconds and you're gonna have to get out and get down. The rotors can flex about four feet either way in this shit."

"Good enough man, and thanks," Brad replied.

Jessica smiled at her cousin. She was scared but exhilarated at the same time. She could see him enjoying the sensation of fear and adrenaline as much as she was and she was just as determined as Brad to find Pete and Charlie. She could hardly wait to get on the ground and begin the search.

Messer swooped down and put the chopper into a tenuous ground hover and yelled, "Go!" as loud as he could, not certain the others had heard him. The five of them shoved their gear out the doors and leapt from the bird to the snow, covering the exposed area of their skins with their arms to keep the rotor wash from causing frostbite. They landed hard within feet of their equipment. The chopper popped up and roared away, leaving only the howling of the wind in their ears.

CHAPTER EIGHT

ON THE SITE

Day 2 1720 hours AKDT

A gust of wind cleared the air for a moment shortly after the team hit their LZ (landing zone). It was eagle-eyed Jared who spotted the wrecked fuselage of the Piper far down below them on the frozen surface of the river, perhaps a hundred meters from the lake that fed the river. The craft had managed to glide only a short distance from where the ELT had been able to send out its last signal, on the east side of Mount Watana.

The snow was still blowing hard, and visibility was extremely limited. They couldn't even shoot a compass bearing to the wreckage. This close to the North Pole, the compass proved useless.

Even with Jared's sighting it was a hard forty-five-minute hike to the wreckage. The terrain was not conducive to walking, and there were patches of deep snow between cracks in the base rock of the mountain that made taking a normal step impossible. It would have been a difficult trek even in summer conditions.

"Spread out and do a three-sixty search," Brad ordered, sending Jessica, Tom, and Jared out in a cloverleaf pattern.

"I hope to hell they got out of this thing before it burned," he muttered, more to himself than to Ving. That was the real reason he'd sent the team searching; if Charlie were in that mess he didn't want Jessica to be the one who found him.

Jessica, Tom, and Jared obediently spread out and commenced to execute the familiar cloverleaf pattern. Jessica had only used it a couple times on her treasure hunt missions, but she was familiar enough with the maneuver to understand Brad's directive.

Brad and Ving approached the blackened and half-melted struts that were all that was left of the fuselage, looking for any sign of life . . . or death, whichever the case might be.

There was no sign of Pete or Charlie, but there were empty cartridge cases scattered everywhere, evidence of a major firefight. "What the fuck happened here?" Brad grumbled. There was a body up close to the fuselage.

"Ving, check his ID," Brad commanded.

Ving approached the body cautiously, although its size reassured him it was not either of his friends. "Sam Henderson, definitely the pilot," Ving replied, kneeling by the frozen body. "Looks like he was badly injured in the crash, but he got out before it burned. No bullet wounds."

There were a lot of tracks, mostly from skis though there were at least two sets of snowshoes.

"I don't like the looks of this." Brad sighed. "What did Pete and Charlie stumble into?" He paused for a second, his mind registering the pattern of the tracks and totaling up the number of personnel who had been there. "Someone came after them," he said finally, indicating the impressions in the snow.

"Yes, and it looks to be a whole damned army," Ving replied. "This just turned into a whole other ball of wax than a search and rescue mission."

"Who were these guys?" Brad asked rhetorically.

"And why were they after Pete and Charlie?" Ving wondered aloud.

"Brad, come and check this out," Jessica yelled. She waited for everyone to approach her and when no one did, she cupped her hands around her mouth and yelled again. This time Brad and the others turned toward her.

The team quickly converged on her position to see what she had discovered.

"Blood in the snow," she said anxiously, "lots of blood."

Jared shouted, "I've got a body over here."

Jessica, Brad, and Ving followed a bloody frozen trail and three sets of tracks nearly forty yards to their left to Jared's position. There lay a body face-planted, half-buried in the snow. There were white cross-country skis on his feet.

Brad reached under the body and rolled it over. There was an M-16 slung around his neck.

"He's just a kid," Brad muttered in disbelief. "Can't be more than sixteen or seventeen."

"Thank God it's not Charlie or Pete," Jessica said with relief.

"I found two more over there," Tom said as he trudged over the ice to join the group. "They're older than this guy, and they're armed with M-16s. Not AR-15s, M-16s with selector switches for full auto. There are two sets of snowshoe tracks with roughly a dozen or so sets of ski tracks heading from here to the northwest.

"Whoever they were, they were in a hell of a hurry. The dead guys not only still had their weapons, but they had a full load of magazines too. The attackers just left them lying there in the snow," Brad said. "Clearly they're not Marines." Everyone knew what he meant. They'd never leave one of their own behind—dead or alive.

"Most likely Pete and Charlie are the ones on snowshoes," Jessica replied. "Charlie hates to ski." Brad wondered if that were true or part of the man's cover story.

"Ving, try to get Robinson on the radio," Brad ordered. "I want to talk to him." He wanted to speak to the man personally, not just to update him on their status but to demand some immediate support. Weather be damned.

Ving knelt out of the wind and fiddled with the radio.

"Tom, we're all good trackers, but you've got far more experience tracking in the snow than the rest of us. Give me your assessment of this site," Brad said.

Tom recited pretty much the same conclusions Brad had already reached. "It looks like someone considered them a serious threat, Brad. I think Pete and Charlie headed northwest around the peak of Mount Watana toward Fog Lakes. Where's the map?" Brad dropped his pack, fished out the map and spread it over his bent knee. Tom studied it for a moment, then indicated the possible route with his index finger. "They're either navigating by terrain association, if they have a map, or they're going on dead reckoning.

"Either way, if they can find Fog Lakes the terrain will be a lot easier than the mountains, and it's pretty much a straight shot down the valley here to Stephan Lake Lodge. Pete would be somewhat familiar with the land between Fog Lakes and Stephan Lake Lodge; he's hunted that country for years."

Brad remembered what Robinson had said regarding the closest place of support near the ELT coordinates being east of Fog Lakes at Stephan Lake, their original destination. He did some measuring with his fingers on the map and estimated approximately eight miles of high country between where they were on Mount Watana down to Fog Lakes, and then another eleven miles of rough country from Fog Lakes to Stephan Lake Lodge. At least Pete and Charlie seemed to be headed in the right direction.

There was another path they might have followed, but Brad knew damned well Pete would never trade ease of travel for shorter distance, especially when being pursued by armed hostiles. He had little choice but to agree with Tom's assessment. A quick glance at Jared who was nodding vigorously, who usually performed the tracking function for the team, showed him that Jared was in full agreement with Tom.

THE TRAIL

"Brad, I'm having serious problems with the ALM radio," Ving said. "I can't reach the trooper office or anyone else. The sat-phone isn't working either. It's almost as if someone is jamming the frequencies." Ving scratched his head. "We're talking some fairly sophisticated equipment here, buddy. This makes no sense. What the hell have we walked into?"

Alaska Land Mobile Radio (ALMR) is a statewide system that connects over one hundred federal, state, and municipal government organizations and first responder entities. The system provides the entities with day-to-day communications and the ability to quickly switch to a communications method that allows them to talk with each other so they can more efficiently communicate in an emergency. Most of the remotely located agencies rely totally on the ALMR as their principal network for daily operations.

A group with the ability to disrupt that network was a disaster in the making. CB radio might still function if those frequencies weren't targeted by the countermeasures, but they would be sorely limited by power constraints. The CB was popular with bush pilots because they operated at such a great height.

"Maybe we just need to move to a different location to get a clear signal," Brad said. "If someone is jamming both of those devices we've got big troubles. If the hostiles have equipment advanced enough to employ electronic warfare countermeasures out here in the Alaskan wilderness then we could be in deep shit for sure."

"We could check the GPS for a shorter route so we might cut them off, but if the sat-phone is jammed I doubt we will pick up the signal from that satellite either," Ving said doubtfully.

Brad stared up into the snow-laden clouds and detected no sign that the increasingly heavy snowfall was going to let up anytime soon. The trail left by Pete, Charlie, and their unknown pursuers appeared glaringly obvious, but he knew that he couldn't afford to tarry too long before following them. The wind was gusting fiercely and the tracks would be obscured by the drifting flakes in short order.

He estimated that they had four to five hours of limited visibility left before the sun gave up and left them in darkness. There was little chance that the moon would be able to peak through the cloud cover, eliminating any possibility of continuing to track them at night. Their options were limited and Brad had to do something quick.

Making a snap decision, he turned to his team. "Check your weapons; make certain your magazines are topped off. We're moving out." Despite the obvious hazards, he was determined to track down Pete and Charlie. Pete was a hell of a man when it came to a firefight, but Charlie was an unknown variable. A dozen men would be too much for Pete to handle alone, especially since he was only carrying his hunting rifle. And if Charlie were injured, which was entirely possible given the blood and number of shell casings they had found, Pete could be at a worse disadvantage than if he were traveling alone.

Brad took the lead and let Jared, who normally would have been the lead tracker, take the rear. Jessica followed right behind him. Ving trailed behind Jessica followed by Tom, pulling the *ahkio*. Stout as Tom was, he was grateful to have three people breaking trail for him. It made the *ahkio* much easier to pull.

Jared followed as far back from Tom and the flat sled as possible, the better to listen for sounds of anyone who might try to track them. There were only five of them, but they were literally loaded for bear. Brad had complete faith that his team, with their training and firepower, could handle the force chasing his friends.

CHAPTER NINE

DISASTER AND DELAY

Day 2 2000 hours AKDT

The Piper had crashed on the frozen river, and when Pete fled he made a beeline northwest, obviously headed for the saddle between Mount Watana and the peak immediately southwest of it. Navigating the terrain proved a grueling task; Pete hadn't made it easy for the men chasing him. Knowing Pete as well as he did, Brad knew that if Pete had known he was being pursed, which he must have, he would make it as difficult as possible for anyone to find him. Brad only hoped Charlie, if he were still alive, were smart enough to shut up and trust Pete's instincts and training.

Brad had been setting a frantic pace for over three hours but made little headway, and he realized without having to glance at his wrist chronometer they had little light left. He followed the trail up over the saddle and started the treacherous descent down a steep draw with a sharp southwest dogleg that would lead to relatively flatter terrain all the way to Fog Lakes. That would then leave them a straight and very familiar trek to Stephan Lake Lodge.

For Brad and company, the path became increasingly difficult. Snow had drifted into the cracks in the stone face of the mountain, and Brad often stopped himself just in time to keep from toppling into a crevice filled with solid appearing snow. He'd warned Jessica repeatedly to stay directly behind him. One wrong step could lead to disaster.

The steep draw turned into a narrow side canyon, and by then Brad could barely make out the outline of a frozen creek at the bottom. The trail led straight down to the creek bank. He called a halt for a short break at a rise in the draw, exhausted from breaking trail but unwilling to admit it.

Ving knew him better than any man alive, and he knew damned well that Brad was flagging and needed a break. "Hey, Tom," he called out, "why don't you let me pull that ahkio for a while?"

Tom squinted ahead and saw that the snow had been blown away from the ground, leaving large rocky bare patches in the snow. He was younger than either Brad or Ving and still felt fairly fresh. It crossed his mind that Ving might be trying to give Brad a rest more than trading off the work, but it didn't matter to him. When Brad was ready to move out again, he would take point for a while. He was a damned good tracker and he knew it.

"I'll take point for a while, Brad, there's not much trail to break, and Ving here is going to play sled dog for a while." Brad acknowledged Tom's suggestion with a nod. It would be a relief to stop breaking trail for a while. He told himself it wasn't so much the physical effort that was sapping his strength but rather the stress of watching for crevices and crannies that were sitting calmly beneath the snow, waiting to trap the unwary trekker.

Brad moved his clenched fist in a circle over his head and then pointed it in the direction he wanted to move. Ving shrugged on the *ahkio* harness and leaned into it, following Brad and Jessica, who in turn followed around twenty meters behind Tom.

As they reached the bottom of the draw, Brad faced a decision. The banks of the frozen creek looked rugged and lined with large, sharp-edged boulders that had broken off the mountain above them and tumbled down to the creek bed. The ice surface of the creek appeared smooth and flat, relatively unobstructed by the big rocks. He knew they carried a risk in taking the easier way, but time appeared short and there was an urgent need to catch up with Pete and Charlie and the men pursuing them.

He took a deep breath and signaled for Tom to follow the frozen surface of the creek the next time the younger man looked back at him. The ice felt solid enough, and it measured almost fifteen feet wide, so when Tom glanced back once more, Brad raised his fist and pumped it up and down, the signal to pick up the pace. Tom moved onto the ice and began moving a hell of a lot faster as the going became easier. The trail seemed to be noticeably fresher, Brad noticed smugly. They were catching up.

A little more than twenty minutes after walking onto the ice, Brad heard the unmistakable sound of cracking. He looked up just in time to see Tom break through the ice and plunge into the icy water beneath. Before he could even begin to run toward Tom, Jessica flashed past him and dove toward the hole in the ice. Tom was spluttering and splashing in the frigid water, and it was clear that the current was trying to drag him under. As Brad launched his body toward the hole, he knew that, short of a miracle, Tom would be sucked under the surface and trapped beneath the ice. He would be lost forever.

Luck was with him, and it was Jessica who provided the miracle. She plunged her arm into the frigid water and managed to tangle her fingers in the straps on the back of Tom's pack. It took every ounce of strength she possessed to maintain her grip on the spluttering Tom, and she was terrified that she would be dragged into the water after him—there was nothing for her to hold on to.

She felt Brad's iron grip on her ankles as he caught her, just as she was about to slip into the water herself. Freed from the moment of the fear she would be dragged in as well, Jessica fearlessly stretched out her other hand and got a handful of Tom's short hair. She was trusting Brad to keep the three of them from slipping into the water. She held onto Tom with all her strength, but she could still feel him starting to slip away from her. The force of the current was hellishly strong and the cold was numbing.

Ving and Jared saved the three of them by the simple expedient of tossing a climbing rope from the *ahkio* to them. His head barely above water, and his arms feeling almost too heavy and too cold to move, Tom grabbed the very end of it, and then Jessica and Brad grabbed it as well. Ving and Jared raced for the creek bank, selecting a slender fir to run the rope behind, and then, using the tree as an anchor, they slowly hauled the three clear of the hole in the ice. Tom was soaked clear through, and the arms of Jessica's parka were soaking wet as well. Brad's parka was wet from lying on the ice and from Jessica and Tom splashing, but the water didn't seep through the thick material.

The entire team was aware that one of the greatest dangers in traveling across the wild country of the Alaskan interior was the risk of falling into open water. Getting wet in sub-zero temperatures was extremely dangerous. Tom had been immersed in the water for less than a minute, but that had been long enough to drop his core body temperature to a life-threatening level. Everyone understood, almost instinctively, what had to be done; it was basic arctic first aid and their training had been the best available.

Jared collected firewood without having to be told, while Jessica broke out one of the silver thermal emergency blankets and wrapped it around Tom's body as he shivered and tried to keep his arms and feet moving. She tore at his wet clothes, knowing he would be better off without them underneath the thermal blanket.

Brad and Ving promptly removed the arctic tent from the ahkio and set it up as Jared knelt in the snow to start a fire with the wood he had collected. Their efforts were smooth and coordinated, each of them aware that there was little time before Tom would start showing signs of hypothermia.

Tom stood over the small fire as Jessica dug through the waterproof bag inside Tom's rucksack for dry clothes. In no time she slipped his wool trousers and shirt on him, not bothering to scrabble in the growing darkness for his spare long johns. The wool socks were harder to get on him, and he had to use one of his own hands to steady himself on her shoulder as she tussled to get them over his stiff, near frozen feet.

His VB boots were wet inside but not soaked. Jessica didn't try to get him to put them on, she simply shed her own parka and stepped close to the shivering Tom and pulled the silver blanket around them both, her body heat helping to warm him.

Darkness fell like a heavy curtain. One second there was minimal visibility, the next there was none. Brad hated having to stop the pursuit, especially since they'd obviously been gaining ground, but reaching Pete and Charlie before dark was now clearly impossible, and probably had been all along. Getting lost or losing the trail in the darkness wouldn't help Pete and Charlie in the least. His only consolation was that he knew Pete's pursuers had to stop too. Traveling after dark with no moon in these conditions was suicide.

They would stay on the creek bank for the night. It was far from an ideal location, but the team had no better options. Brad was concerned that the trail might disappear overnight, but he knew that Tom would need to bring his body heat back up, and for that they would need shelter.

Getting an early start in the morning was now even more important. They would have to break camp in the dark and get moving at daybreak. The longer it took to catch up the worse their chances for success would be. They had been so close! This major setback was a huge disappointment, but Brad took comfort and pride in knowing he and his team had saved Tom's life.

Jared built a huge fire, and he and Ving had been busy collecting enough firewood to last through the night.

Brad, Ving and Jared huddled around the fire as Jessica took Tom inside the arctic tent and rolled out the thick down sleeping bag.

"There," she said, "is that better?"

Tom, his face blue, his body still shivering and his teeth still chattering, tried to answer her, but he couldn't get the words out. Jessica frowned at the man she had known for far less time than she'd known either Ving or Jared and made a decision.

She peeled off her outer clothes, down to her wool long johns, and crawled into the sleeping bag with the muscular Tom, wrapping her arms around him and sharing her body warmth. "If you get a hard-on I'm climbing out of this sleeping bag, damn you!" she whispered. She couldn't see it in the darkness inside the tent, but Tom's grin spread all the way across his face.

"I want to be moving at first light," Brad said outside the tent, but loud enough for Jessica and Tom to hear him. The light from the fire flickered and cast shadows on his face. "They have to be stopped for the night, too, there's no way they could move in this shit at night."

Ving said nothing. He knew they would have to find Pete and Charlie as soon as possible. Pete was a hell of a warrior, but Charlie remained an unknown, and Ving wasn't any more comfortable with that than Brad. Wordlessly, he and Jared prepared a meal from the MREs in the ahkio. There was plenty for all of them. When it was hot, Brad carried two of them inside the squad tent to give to

Tom and Jessica, though the tin cup of coffee Ving had made so carefully was rather cold by the time he got inside.

"Caught you in bed with my cousin, didn't I?" he teased.

Tom clawed at the zipper on the sleeping bag, struggling to escape, but Jessica stopped him. "He's just teasing you," she said quietly, just before she faced Brad and sat up. "That was mean."

Brad just grinned at her and passed her the two meals.

Ving kept trying to raise someone on the radio and the sat-phone, but he had no luck at all. In a few minutes, he sent Jared inside, taking the first watch outside the tent himself.

CHAPTER TEN

SHOOTER

Day 3 0500 hours AKDT

Brad had the last watch, and it fell to him to go inside the tent to wake the others. He fumbled around in the darkness and finally found a shoulder to shake, whereupon he spoke in a loud voice, startling all of them out of a sound sleep. "Let's get a move on, people! Time to saddle up and move out." His chronometer said 0500 sharp, and he was eager to get moving.

Knowing he wouldn't need to tell them twice, Brad moved out of the tent and back to the fire, where the tin cup holding his instant coffee water was bubbling merrily in the freezing cold. It was still about an hour and a half before sunrise, but they needed to break camp and repack the *ahkio. We'll catch those bastards today!*

Tom awakened warm and cozy and immediately turned onto his side in the futile hope that Jessica had not noticed the rigid lump in his wool trousers.

Jessica smiled in the darkness. It was not the first time a man had reacted to her that way, and even though she really believed that her heart belonged to Charlie Dawkins, she was flattered. *Don't get too cocky, girl. He's a man, and they're all like that. You could have been a ninety-year-old hag and he still would have been like that when he woke up!* She liked Tom, and she didn't want to embarrass him, so she crawled out of the sleeping bag and got dressed quickly without saying a word.

They moved out almost immediately, continuing down the narrow river canyon, sticking to the banks to avoid risking another breakthrough on the icy creek. It was slower going, but there had been little additional snowfall during the night and Brad felt relieved that they were still able to follow the trail. The canyon widened as they dropped in elevation and the frozen creek got bigger as several feeder streams from small side canyons and draws fed into the main flow.

As the canyon grew wider, they encountered more and more level ground. The forest became a little denser, but there was still plenty of snow on the ground. Despite the forecasts they had received from the Weather Service and from Ben Robinson, the weather cleared and they could actually see the majestic peak of Mount Watana rising up behind them.

As they continued to follow the trail, Brad spotted a dog sled team and a lone man emerging from one of the larger side canyons, making straight for them. The man appeared alone and he didn't look dangerous, but Brad was taking no chances. He ordered the team to move into defensive positions while he remained standing, his rifle draped over his forearm. He had no way of knowing if the man was affiliated with the men chasing Pete and Charlie, but he was going to play it safe.

"Keep an eye on him, Ving," Brad muttered, just loud enough to be heard. He put a smile on his face and waited patiently for the man to draw closer.

All of them could hear the sled driver calling out commands to his dogs, and the animals were barking loudly. Brad didn't know if they always did that or if they were happy to see him.

The sled seemed to move almost recklessly fast as it approached, but the man obviously retained tight control over the dogs.

"Hello the camp!"

Brad could not even make a guess at the man's age, covered as he was in shapeless but very colorful arctic clothing. Brad raised a hand in greeting, but he didn't speak.

"Gee! Whoa!" The man stopped the dogs, and they suddenly came to a complete standstill roughly fifty feet from where Brad was standing. The runners on the sled threw up a rooster tail of fine powdered snow as the musher skidded it to a stop.

There was a rifle resting in a scabbard strapped to one handle on the sled, but it was strictly a sporting rifle, not one of military design. The musher made no effort to reach for the weapon. He didn't seem offended or surprised that Brad hadn't spoken to him. He simply stepped off the runners of the sled and walked up to kneel by his lead dog, patting it affectionately and talking to it as if the animal were human.

Sensing no immediate threat from the peculiar stranger, Brad approached the man. The musher looked massive. Brad guessed him to be at least seven feet tall, and his shoulders had to be as wide as an axe handle. A long beard, grizzly brown with touches of gray, covered most of his face and the skin that was exposed had the leathery look of a hard living mountain man in his fifties.

Brad offered his hand. "I'm Brad Jacobs."

"You fellers from the outside?" the man asked as he extended his enormous hand.

"Outside?"

The man laughed a deep, chesty laugh. "You ain't from around these parts. Look to be from the lower forty-eight."

"That's right. We're from Texas."

"They call me Shooter. Franklin 'Shooter' Hall to put a point to it."

"What can I do for you, Shooter?"

The big, rough man gave Brad an appraising look and then took in the tense faces of the rest of the team.

"I spotted you when I came outta Spook Canyon back there an' I thought I'd best stop by to warn you." Brad could detect no guile in the big man's eyes, but he got the distinct impression that, despite his country bumpkin manner, Franklin "Shooter" Hall was a very intelligent man.

"Warn us about what?"

"I'll get to that in a minute," Shooter said, eying the *ahkio*. "I'm feelin' kinda wolfish, you boys got any grub? I ain't et since day before yesterday, been holed up at the north end of Spook Canyon, cussin' myself for getting surprised by that blackbird storm like some kinda durned *cheechako*."

Brad was in a hurry, but he sensed that whatever this man had to say was important and he couldn't afford to ignore him or offend him. He knew little about the mountain men who chose to live their lives away from civilization except that they tended to fall into two categories: men who simply couldn't abide by the restrictions and trappings of society, and men who had a problem coexisting with the law. He was wise enough to recognize that there were also men who had simply slipped between the cracks, men who fit messily into both categories. Men who would be ignored by society and pardoned by the law if they chose the quiet, almost invisible existence of living off the grid.

In either case, solitary men were apt to be garrulous when they crossed paths with another human being; the coin of exchange was pleasant conversation, and, of course, the sharing of food. Even the crustiest of old curmudgeons up here would share whatever they had with a stranger. They possessed a real appreciation of life on the jagged edge, and they never knew when they might depend on the generosity of others. It was an unwritten code based on the concept of karma that boiled down to a simple sophomoric expression: *What goes around comes around.*

They had broken camp in the cold predawn, munching energy bars and drinking hot instant coffee. Despite his impatience to keep after Pete and Charlie, Brad sensed that this mountain man knew something . . . something of vital importance to the mission. And however long it took him to share the information was going to be time well spent. First Robinson and then Messer had clammed up about something in these mountains, something they really didn't seem to want any outsider to know. In all likelihood, Shooter was going to tell him all about it. He turned and waved in the team, introducing them each in turn. Shooter was astonished to find that Jessica was a woman, and the mountain man seemed mightily impressed with her.

"We're going to stop and have a little breakfast," Brad explained, "and Shooter here will be our guest. I thought we'd break out some of the good stuff because our friend here is feeling, as he puts it, 'wolfish'."

Jessica knew the urgency of their pursuit, and she understood her cousin well enough to know that he needed something from this older man or they wouldn't be taking this precious time to gab with Shooter and share food with him. She forced herself to curb her impatience and gave Shooter her most dazzling smile. She was a team player and she would use any weapon in her arsenal to get Pete and Charlie back.

"I think I can rustle something up, if Jared will help me. We don't have much other than MREs, but I know a few tricks to make them taste a little better," Jessica said, twirling her hair with her fingers. "I'll make you think you're at a Michelin-rated restaurant." She winked at Shooter.

Shooter laughed a big, booming sound that echoed through the valley. "I'll just bet you will!"

Ving and Tom set out gathering firewood as Jessica and Jared rummaged through the *ahkio* for the rations and water.

"It's gonna be a crimpy day," Shooter said, his eyes still on the golden hair Jessica had freed from the confines of her parka. "We allus git these really cold days after a blackbird storm like we had last night." He turned his eyes back to Brad and the shrewd look in them told Brad that Shooter was doing a little internal evaluation of his own. "You boys look to be pretty well prepared for this country. You got the look of some kind of soldiers, except for the lady of course. You military or ex-military?" The question was within the bounds of propriety, but Brad sensed that the time for games was over.

"Most of us are retired Marines," Brad answered. Despite his need to be candid, he was reluctant to tell this man they had been Special Operators in Force Recon.

"What's your business out here?"

"We're on a search and rescue mission for two friends of ours. Their plane crashed on the east side of the mountain day before yesterday."

Shooter frowned. "You boys are on the wrong side of the mountain."

"I know that," Brad said patiently. "We tracked them here along with a force of nearly a dozen men we think are pursuing them. You wouldn't happen to have any idea who they might be, would you?"

"As a matter of fact, that's what I stopped to warn you about. You fellers are about to enter Aryan territory. If I was you, I'd turn around and go back the way you came."

"We won't be leaving without our friends," Brad said with a look of grim determination. "What do you mean *Aryan territory*?"

"Aryan Nations. They control the territory from this mountain to the west end of Fog Lakes where

Fog Creek enters the Susitna River. And they don't cotton to strangers."

"I thought this was a state wilderness area."

"Alaska's a big place, fella. Lots of oddball people living here that think they have a better claim on the land they live on than the gov'ment does. They ain't enough troopers to do anything about it . . . and the gov'ner, well, he ain't about to call out the National Guard unless them folks gets too far outta line."

"How well do you know these people?"

"Well enough to stay outta their territory and mind my own bi'ness. We kinda got an agreement. I don't go any farther west than this mountain and they leave me the hell alone to trap, hunt or do whatever I please. I got a feeling they're hiding something big down in that valley and they're the type that don't mind a little killing if it suits their purposes. I've only spoken with them a few times, but they definitely seem to be a paranoid bunch. If they think your friends mighta seen whatever they're hiding from that plane before it crashed, I 'spect they would hunt them down to protect their secret." He rubbed his chin for a moment. "Any of you reckon that these Aryan fellas might be the *reason* your friends' plane went down?"

"What aren't you telling me, friend?" Brad's voice took on the tone of a poker player about to lay his hand out on the table face up.

Shooter had obviously made up his mind concerning the little group.

"From what I can tell, they're a white supremacist neo-Nazi militant group that got run out of Idaho a couple years back. Call themselves the Order of Phineas or some such outlandish thing. A bunch of domestic terrorists if you ask me. They're led by a man name of Lewis Hostback. He claims to be the last living ordained pastor of the Aryan Nations. They're a real special breed."

Brad was having trouble processing all this new information at once. He'd never stopped to consider that anything but weather or mechanical failure could have brought down the plane. And now he had to contend with a bunch of racist motherfuckers who would not take kindly to his big, black friend Ving or his pretty white cousin, Jessica. His background had prepared him to expect surprises, but this was definitely a much bigger problem than he'd anticipated.

"Word is there's a bunch of 'em living down in that valley. Nobody knows for sure exactly how many, at least nobody that lived to talk about it. But rumor is a couple hundred."

Brad recalled his conversation with Ben Robinson in Talkeetna, when he asked for the names of any local residents in the search area who might be willing to lend assistance. He had known it was a remote region, but he'd definitely felt something was amiss when Robinson said he could not recommend even a single person to assist in the search mission. Combined with the information Shooter had just given him, it was all starting to make sense.

CHAPTER ELEVEN

PUSHING ON

Day 3 0830 hours AKDT

After Shooter had eaten and bid them farewell, the realization of their situation smacked Brad in the face. He was a confident and well-trained man, accustomed to dealing with whatever obstacles or enemies he encountered, but this was so far beyond the scope of his capability and that of his little team that he was staggered. He had entered his trusted friends into a game where the opposition had morphed from a dozen or so players into an army—a well-armed, organized army with experienced soldiers of its own who targeted innocent people as the enemy.

He had read about Aryan Nations and other white-supremacist groups, just as he had read up on every radical militant group the media wrote about. Despite their nutcase cause, Aryan Nations was no collection of fly-by-night lunatics. Among their ranks could be found special operators and disenchanted military types, men and women who had a working knowledge of real combat, strategy, communications, demolitions, and a host of other skills required to become proficient in the arts of war.

He found himself suddenly and deeply concerned regarding the safety of his team. There was still no question that he would continue the rescue operation for Pete and Charlie. They were his responsibility; one his character would not permit him to shirk. The game had changed, though. He was facing a far larger and more capable force than he had imagined, and the team he had brought with him was only prepared for search and rescue. He wondered if he should send them home and continue alone.

No matter how it was handled, Brad could see only a thin sliver of possibility he might survive this mission, and the others, especially Jessica, hadn't signed on for that. He pulled Ving aside to get some feedback from his trusted friend.

Ving had finished repacking the *ahkio* and was fastening the bindings on his snowshoes. Jessica, Tom, and Jared were laughing and joking quietly almost twenty-five feet away, kicking snow over the flames of the fire.

"You had any luck reaching the troopers with the radio?"

"Nope," Ving responded sourly. "Still jammed."

Now that he had a better idea of what they were facing, Brad was forced to agree with Ving's assumption that electronic signal jamming countermeasures were being employed in this desolate but beautiful part of Alaska.

"We could certainly use their support right now," Brad said, with a worried look. "The storm has passed and the weather is clearing up. They should be looking for us by now."

"Yeah, they probably are, but we're quite a ways from the ELT coordinates. They've got a hell of an area to cover and unless the trail miraculously remains up there on that windswept plateau, they ain't gonna have any idea which way we've gone."

"I agree, buddy. We need to back up and regroup, reconsider our plan of attack . . . if we even need one anymore."

There was something Ving detected in Brad's voice he'd never heard before, and they had waded through some seriously deep shit together many times in the past.

"Reorganize and regroup" was a military principle that was the cornerstone of Brad and Ving's success, both in the military and on their private missions since.

"We are a force of five, well-armed but with a very limited supply of ammo. We're facing a well-armed force of around a dozen, but who we have now learned have considerable reinforcement assets down in that valley." Brad's finger pointed in the direction they had been headed.

"As I see it, we have two options. We can maintain our pursuit or pull back to the crash site where we can hopefully make contact with the state troopers for additional support. After talking with Shooter, I'm pretty well convinced that the first option is going to send us all to a frozen and unmarked grave." He gave Ving a frank stare. "What do you think?" Brad asked.

"My gut says we need to keep pushing on, Brad, but my head says you don't want to lead your entire team into a suicide mission."

"That's my concern. We both know that the longer it takes to find Pete and Charlie the worse their chance of survival. I'm not sure we can risk wasting any time trying to get help…. I'm not even sure anybody *will* help. From what Ben Robinson said in Talkeetna, most of their manpower out here is from volunteer search groups. Those volunteer groups will not be prepared to help us on an armed assault mission."

"So, what's your question?" Ving asked with a wide grin. He had no intention of abandoning the rescue effort. Leaving Pete and Charlie was not to be considered, whatever the cost, personal danger be damned. He would walk into hell for Pete or anyone else on the team . . . they had done it for him.

Brad smiled. He'd known Ving's answer before he'd asked. He'd just wanted to make sure they were in agreement. He knew the clock was ticking and they had to reach Pete fast if he was to have any chance of making it out alive. While waiting for reinforcements seemed prudent, it just wasn't going to work in this situation.

His biggest concern was Jessica. The rest of his team were trained veterans who knew the risks, or would when they were explained to them, and would accept them or pull out. But even though Jessica's own exploits routinely put her at risk, this was different. Brad felt responsible for her. When he had agreed to let her come along, this was only supposed to be a search and rescue mission involving her boyfriend, hazardous but not unreasonable.

Unfortunately for all of them, the search and rescue mission had ballooned into something entirely different and now he was regretting his decision to bring her along, but there was no way to exclude her at this point. There was, simply, no safe place to send her. Their chance for a successful search and rescue had been greatly compromised. Brad knew what he had to do. He didn't like it, but there was a chance that, with his team's help, there might be a way to survive this disaster.

DAY 3 1030 hours AKDT

Taking point once more, Brad moved quickly, following the trail down the canyon. They dropped over a thousand feet in elevation and the snow gave way to large open areas of stone and soil. The terrain changed dramatically from the wide open spaces on the mountain top to a thick forest canopy.

They still traveled single file with Jessica right on Brad's heels. Because of the added concealment afforded by the forest, his instincts and training forced him to consider the likelihood of an ambush.

"Tom, take Jessica to the rear," Brad commanded. "Ving and Jared, move up on my six." If they were attacked, he didn't want his cousin at the front of the line.

Less than half an hour later, gunfire erupted around them. "Down!" Brad whisper yelled. He spun around as he hit the ground to make sure that Jessica was safe. Tom was shielding her body with his and the five of them searched for cover that would stop the hail of bullets coming at them. Instead of just concealment, cover blocks bullets, concealment only hides you. The team scrambled desperately for good cover as the incoming gunfire increased in intensity from several enemies and multiple vantage points.

Brad went to ground behind a large fallen tree. The adrenaline rush from the firefight was a familiar sensation, and he was acutely aware of elation rising inside him. They had caught up with the people who were chasing Pete and Charlie! He had total confidence in his team's ability to handle this ambush, but he was a little puzzled at the size of it.

As best he could figure, they were taking fire from perhaps six shooters, and there should have been more. They had been following a trail made by a dozen men, at least. He stopped thinking about the mystery and returned fire, all the while looking for any sign of Pete and Charlie.

Ving and Jared were firing methodically at muzzle flashes and smoke. Brad glanced back up the trail for Jessica and spotted her as she peeked over a large boulder, taking carefully placed shots.

"Easy on the ammo!" Tom called out just as Jessica's last shot struck home and elicited a blood-curdling death yell from the man she'd hit.

"Too late," she said, pulling the trigger and only getting a clicking sound. "I think I'm out. What do I do now?"

"Get down and stay put," Tom said. "You're safe behind that rock."

"No way. I can shimmy over there and get more ammo," Jessica said.

"Don't even think about it," Brad said. He'd taken cover closer to her so he could keep an eye on her and continue the defensive assault. "We didn't come all the way out here to save Pete and your boyfriend only to have you get killed."

Jessica didn't respond. She just shrank behind the rock and curled herself as small as she could make herself.

"At least your last shot was a kill shot," Tom remarked as he caught sight of a shadowy figure who hadn't fully considered the difference between cover, which stopped bullets, and concealment, which didn't. In this case, the difference got him killed.

Jared grunted as his first shot struck home, taking off the top of one attacker's head. The boom of the big Barrett sounded like thunder in the forest, and the sound of the shot overshadowed the "pop, pop, pop" of the 5.56mm rounds from the ambushers' M-16s and the team's M4A1s.

The firefight continued for the next ten minutes, sporadic gunfire breaking out followed by several seconds of silence. Sweat dripped down Brad's face, despite the frigid temperature. He took shots as he thought about why there seemed to be so few enemies returning fire. From what Shooter had told him and what Messer had implied, there should have been dozens of combatants firing on them. Ving low crawled over to Brad's log.

"Something's not right about this," Brad whispered when Ving crawled up beside him. Ving's breathing was even, and Brad wondered if he'd ever seen the man truly rattled.

"What? That we're winning?" Ving asked with a vicious grin spread over his lips. "Hang on." He picked up his weapon and aimed. "Here comes another." He fired and another man dropped. Brad hadn't even seen him until he was dead on the frozen ground. "We are winning, you know."

"It's too easy. I only count three more enemy weapons firing on us and we've been tracking a force of at least a dozen men. I think their leader got smart; this is a delaying force pure and simple. I'll bet you anything that these guys disengage in a minute or two and leave us hiding behind cover. I'd guess that son of a bitch, Hostback, is going for reinforcements. He may be hoping these guys take us out, but if not he'll be ready for us. I'm telling you. They're more of them somewhere. And they're ready for us." The initial adrenaline rush at finally catching up to these men and possibly rescuing their friends was slowly replaced with the bitter realization that this mission just continued to get harder and harder with no end in sight.

Ving put down his weapon and realized it was eerily quiet. "Shit. Do you hear that?" Both men picked up their heads and were silent for a moment.

"Yep. It's too quiet. See—they're retreating."

"Exactly. The sound of silence is not a good thing here. You're right. This isn't over and I think they're smarter than we may have thought."

"Right. We need to—" But another round of bullets littered the air and the men quickly reloaded and returned fire.

They finished off the remaining shooters, Jared taking out the last one with a clean head shot. The shooter's head popped up to check on them, just like a turkey in a box at a turkey shoot back home. Jared's aim was slightly off. The massive .50 caliber round missed the bridge of the man's nose and entered his left eye, leaving a gaping crater in the back of his skull, though his face seemed unscathed.

One shooter was still alive, squirming on the ground trying to hold his entrails in with his hands. A three-round burst had caught him in the belly and there was nothing anyone could do for him. Brad and his team watched and waited. No one came out of the forest to help the man. Nor was there any more shooting.

"We're clear," Brad said. "Let's get moving again."

Staying low to the ground, Jessica ran from behind her rock to where Brad and the others were. "What?" she asked, staring at the man who was bleeding out and making awful gurgling noises. "We can't just leave him, can we?"

Tom cocked his rifle. "You're right." He grinned. "I guess we can put him out of his misery."

Ving grabbed the gun's muzzle and aimed it at the ground. "No way. We have no idea how many of these idiots are out there and what they have in store. We can't afford to waste any ammo. Not even one round.

Tom's grin faded. "You're right." He turned to the figure on the ground, who was still breathing. But he was struggling to take in air.

Jessica stepped forward. "I'm serious. We can't just leave him." She squatted next to the soldier and moved his hair off his forehead. "Look at him. He's just a kid. At least let me see what we have in the first-aid kit." She stood up and scrambled to the pack containing the medical supplies.

Brad stood over the bleeding man. "Band-Aids ain't gonna help. Let's not waste any more time or supplies here."

Jessica pulled out an ampule of morphine and a syringe. She filled it up and knelt by the boy again. "Come on, Brad. Let me put this kid out of his misery. It won't save him, but it will take away his pain."

"No way." Brad stepped forward, glancing between Ving and Jared. "We're Marines. We've been trained to defend our country, our comrades and ourselves at any cost. Part of that is killing, if necessary. I'm not letting you take a life. Even if it is out of mercy." He held out his hand. "Let me do it."

Jessica stared at her cousin. "Brad. You gave me a high-powered rifle. I've been firing at people for twenty minutes. I'm cool. My only concern is getting back Charlie and Pete. It's pretty clear from the trail and how pissed off these guys seem to be that they survived the plane crash."

The boy on the ground lifted his head. "Plane crash?" he asked. "You're looking for them?"

"Yes! Yes!" Jessica said. "Are they alive? Have you seen them? Which way did they go? Why are you people after them? They just came here to hunt bear. Why are you hunting them?"

"Hunted," the boy said, his voice barely audible. "We captured them." His eyes lost focus and he died before anyone had a chance to inject him with the opioid.

CAUGHT!

Day 3 1100 hours AKDT

Lewis Hostback and his remaining six men surrounded Pete and Charlie as they rushed for one of the Order's small guard outposts at the bottom of Mount Watana. "Try to run, and I'll kill you now," Hostback said, aiming his rifle at Pete's head. "Come with us and maybe we'll let you live a little longer."

Pete and Charlie were casual friends who'd talked mostly about hunting. Pete had noticed that every time he asked Charlie about his past, all he got were evasive and vague answers. Now he needed Charlie to understand his silent cues and play along.

"We'll cooperate," Pete told Hostback. "Just tell us what you want and we can arrange it. Money. Supplies. Whatever you need."

Hostback hit Pete's shoulder with his weapon. "We need to eradicate the enemy. Now shut up and get in front of us. Let's go." Pete and Charlie exchanged looks and made their way to the front of the group. They started down the mountain.

"We found them, you know," Hostback said to Pete's back. Pete's stomach tightened. "Oh yeah? Who's that?"

"Your friends. I guess they came looking for you. We found them while pursuing you."

Pete knew Brad and Ving would come for them. But he had no way of knowing if Hostback was bluffing. "Then where the hell are they?" Pete asked.

"My guess is dead. When we got to the south end of the creek, me and my guys took you and I sent the rest of my guys to ambush your little search party."

Pete was doing the math in his head—trying to figure out how many enemy combatants they were up against. He looked around and counted five people including the one the others had been calling Lewis. "Good luck to them," Pete said confidently. "Three of your guys could not take out even one Marine."

"Too bad there were six of them."

Pete exhaled. Brad, Ving and whoever else they'd brought could definitely handle six of these fools. He put his head down and kept walking.

Hostback pushed his men down the mountain. A shot rang out and everyone stopped. For a moment, Pete thought he could figure out whose rifle it was just from the sound of it firing. "Hope you said goodbye to your friends before you left," Hostback said smugly. "My guys don't miss."

Neither do mine, Pete thought.

"So let me ask you this," Pete said. He'd learned in the Corps that keeping an enemy talking could do two things. First, it could make him slip up and say something that could help neutralize the situation. Second, it always bought him time. "Why ambush my guys and kill them if you just captured us?"

Lewis Hostback knew these two interlopers would not be alive in twenty-four hours. So he supposed it didn't matter what he said now. "I don't give a fuck what happens to them. I gave kill orders, but I just needed to slow them down." He hoped his hasty ambush would either stop or slow down whoever was chasing him long enough for him to get reinforcements. He hadn't expected a search and rescue team to show up so quickly after the storm. He definitely hadn't expected them to be armed or well trained. It was clear from the speed and tenacity of his pursuers that they meant business . . . and Lewis felt the first tendrils of fear clutch at his heart.

The Order had come so far and they were finally beginning to see real profits from their illegal mining enterprise. They were actually within sight of attaining their first goal—amassing enough capital to fund their ultimate mission. In a year, perhaps less, they would have enough funds to take the Order back to the lower forty-eight, where they could reassert their dominance over the Aryan Brotherhood and begin to take their holy message to the masses. They weren't going to let two hapless hunters screw up what they'd worked so hard to accomplish.

Lewis believed that if he could just reach the small guard outpost at the bottom of the mountain he would be able to set up another roadblock, leaving a couple more men with the two guards there to slow down his stalkers long enough for him to reach reinforcements. Based on the controlled, steady fire he heard behind him, it was a good assumption that the men he left behind at the lower guard shack would be a human sacrifice. It was just as possible that the lengthy gunfire meant his men had taken out the crash victims' friends, but he would rather think about the worst-case scenario and then be pleasantly surprised. If the search party had been eliminated by his guys, then he could reunite with his men at the guard outpost and do away with his hostages then. No need to worry about possible courses of action until he knew exactly what he was dealing with.

That was okay with him, provided he survived to continue the Order's mission. He was completely convinced that without him to lead them, the Order of Phineas would crumble immediately. God himself had anointed Lewis Hostback to lead it. Lewis knew that because God had told him so. God had spoken and Lewis had listened.

The gunfire eventually faded and Lewis and his men pushed Pete and Charlie down the mountain. When they reached the guard shack, Lewis approached his prisoners with his gun in his hand.

"Look," Pete said. "If you let us go now, no harm no foul. You haven't hurt anyone. We don't know anything. We only came here to go on a hunting trip. It was just a matter of—"

Lewis hit him on the side of his head with the butt of his rifle. "Shut up or I'll kill you now." He motioned to his number-two guy. "Take care of them," he said, then walked away to talk to the guys he'd sent ahead down the mountain.

The thin, blond man unlocked a closet door to the side of the shack and motioned Pete and Charlie in. Once they got in, the man retied their hands and feet. They heard someone lock the door and Lewis summoning his men.

"We still have more work to do," Lewis said. "I think we can assume the men we sent to find the search party did not make it out of that combat situation."

"Let them not have died in vain!" a man shouted. "The wrath of God Almighty will rain down of those who have harmed us. No soul shall escape God's will. Especially those who have caused irreparable harm to the Order of Phineas."

"Are you listening to this shit?" Pete whispered to Charlie. "I guess there are holy rollers among us." It was too dark in the closet to see Charlie's reaction, but Pete imagined he was rolling his eyes.

* * *

"Why do you think we're still here?" Charlie asked.

Of the two, Pete was by far the more seasoned soldier. He knew very little about Charlie but got the feeling from him that there was something about him he didn't want Pete to know. From his years in the armed forces, Pete knew that not all servicemen and women liked to talk about their past. Maybe Charlie was one of the disenfranchised.

"Clearly the leader of these skinhead freaks think we can do something for him."

"Like what?"

"Your guess is as good as mine. Maybe he thinks we know something or that we were sent here to spy on him and his operation."

"Yeah, probably. Or maybe he wants to know if we've told anyone about what they're doing up here in the middle of nowhere."

"How could we tell anyone?" Pete wondered. "We don't even know what's going on."

"All I know is that my shoulders ache like hell and I'm losing feeling in my hands."

"You and me both, brother." Pete tried to keep his tone level as he said that as to not give away what he was really thinking. He had no proof, but after years of interrogating people and conducting interviews, he had learned to pick up on the most subtle verbal and nonverbal cues. Like how Charlie was much too quick to respond to Pete's statement and how he deflected. It made Pete think that Charlie knew more than he was saying.

Charlie knew precisely who Lewis Hostback was, and he had a good idea what Lewis was doing up here in the Alaskan interior. What he didn't know was the mechanism that Hostback was employing to achieve his goal of taking the Order of Phineas back to Coeur d'Alene or how they intended to pay for it.

He felt bad about deceiving Jessica, her cousin Brad, and Brad's team; they were good people, the best. Something had happened between Jessica and he, something he neither intended nor planned on. Now his own heart hurt because of his deceit. He could only hope he survived this so he could tell her the truth, but first he had a mission. He forced his mind back to the words Lewis was saying.

* * *

"I think we should kill them right now, Pastor Hostback," Simon Killian said.

Lewis looked at Killian with veiled contempt. He needed this moron and the thugs he had brought with him from Coeur d'Alene. He used them as his own 'Gestapo,' an organization he had studied and admired for years. He had very skillfully employed the Gestapo's tactics over the past two years to preserve the secrets of the Order of Phineas and subtly keep the membership in line.

"We need them, Simon," Lewis said firmly. "These men are Feds, and we can't afford to kill them until we know what they've passed on to their ZOG masters. It's also possible that we might need them as hostages if they've alerted anyone what we're doing up here. I don't have to tell you what would happen if the ZOG discovered our mining operation on these 'public' lands."

"Yes, Pastor. Your words make perfect sense," Simon conceded. "We must protect our gold mines at all costs."

There was a murmur of agreement among the men Lewis had gathered in the relative warmth of the log hut, and Lewis knew he had won, at least for the moment.

* * *

Charlie began to work his hands, loosening the bonds the Phineas creeps had tied him with. He had employed an old yoga trick to keep them from binding him as tightly as they thought they had. He'd made his fingers as wide as he could and flattened his hands so when he tensed his muscles, the binds were loose enough for him to shimmy out of. There was no time to spare. He had to get loose and make his way to Fog Lakes.

There was a decommissioned satellite station for the Extremely Low Frequency radio facility on Adak Island there, and Charlie planned to use it to contact his superiors, since ELF radio transmissions were almost impossible to jam.

The ELF equipment required massive amounts of electricity, and there was no longer power to the abandoned facility, but his mission briefing had included the secrets of a simple device called a discharge capacitor, and there were discharge capacitors at Fog Lakes which collected static electricity from the atmosphere and could power the ELF gear. Normally, the Navy sent a team of engineers up to Fog Lakes every couple of years to release the charge so the damned things didn't self-destruct. They hadn't been sent this year. The agency had some very long arms.

"Pete!" Charlie hissed.

"Yeah?" Pete answered, very quietly. He didn't fancy being slapped around anymore by Simon and his thugs.

"I've just about gotten my hands free, but I don't think it makes any sense to try to overpower these freaks here. I'm pretty sure the leader's going to take us with him when he leaves those poor suckers behind. I think we'll have a better chance of escaping when we've got fewer people watching us."

"Cool," Pete said, finally hooking his thumb through one of the ropes and easing it down his palm. "I'm sure it's Brad and Ving tracking these bastards down. I swear I recognized the sound of Jared's Barrett in that firefight."

That sounded rather farfetched to Charlie, but there was no time to argue, and, besides, Pete had a way of knowing certain things that was downright spooky. If it helped him to believe Brad and company were coming to their rescue, Charlie was all for it. As for himself, he was determined to get to Fog Lakes.

CHAPTER TWELVE

CLOSING IN

Day 3 1800 hours AKDT

There were still two hours of daylight left when Jared, still running point, came rushing back to Brad and the others with his hand raised in the sign for a halt. He had been searching nearly a hundred meters in front of the team when he spotted the smoke coming from a chimney. He paused for a moment, unsure of what he was looking at. Then he carefully made his way through the snow a few more meters until he saw a log cabin.

He had hidden behind a half-submerged boulder and watched the sole sentry, armed with an M-16, for just a few minutes before the cabin door opened and a replacement came out. He could see only one other man through the open door, and the cabin was really just one room with a kind of lean-to shack of rough planks built against the back wall, probably storage for supplies.

Jared knelt close to Brad, who had also taken a knee, and quickly explained what he had found. "I watched the cabin and its occupants for several minutes. I'm not sure, but so far, I've only seen two of them. Both armed, of course. Both move like soldiers. But there's something about them that makes me think they weren't trained in the traditional sense. I can't put my finger on it. But they seem . . . rogue. I didn't see any sign of Pete or Charlie. But I can't say with certainty that they're not being held inside somewhere."

Brad moved off to one side behind a stand of firs and beckoned to Ving, Tom, and Jessica to join them. They gathered around and listened intently while Brad spoke. "Ordinarily I'd just bypass these guys, but like Jared said, we have no way of knowing whether they've got Pete and Charlie inside or not. What we're going to do is have Jared create a diversion and try to draw the men in the cabin outside. It isn't much of a plan, but it's the best we can do at the moment. Any questions?"

"So we think they're still alive?" Jessica asked.

"We go on that assumption until we have proof to the contrary."

They spread out and began to move toward the cabin.

* * *

"Hello the camp!" Jared called out, unconsciously mimicking Shooter's earlier greeting. He was hobbling pitifully and holding his hand against the front of his parka. Inside the jacket, he concealed Ving's M4A1, which was much easier to hide. Ving had temporary custody of his Barrett. Brad, watching from approximately fifty meters away, was impressed with Jared's acting ability.

"I'm hurt.... Please . . . help me!" Jared allowed his voice to trail off, and the sentry rapidly came to port arms and moved closer, though he maintained a suspicious distance.

"What the hell happened to you?" the sentry called out.

"Grizzly," Jared sobbed. "Big one . . . Killed all of my friends . . . Help me! I think my ribs are crushed...." Jared fell forward into the snow, facing away from the sentry. Brad could clearly see him taking the M4A1 out of his open parka and readying it.

"Dillon, Max!" the sentry shouted over his shoulder. "Get Ron and bring the first aid kit, we've got a man down out here!" It was a rookie mistake, but anyone might have fallen for it. The sentry rushed toward Jared's prone figure.

The sentry reached Jared just as the cabin door burst open and three men came running out, weapons at the ready. "No!" one of them screamed at the sentry, raising his rifle and taking aim at Jared.

The massive boom of Jared's Barrett broke the still, frigid air. The man who had aimed at Jared toppled to the ground, his chest a bloody mess, a hole where his ribs should have been. The startled sentry tried to bring his M-16 to bear on Jared. A burst from the M4A1 in Jared's hands stopped him cold. The other two fell just as swiftly. Jared lay still for a moment and then decided his would-be attackers were dead.

Brad ran to see if Jared was all right. He dropped to his knees and slipped his arm around Jared's shoulders. "You good?" he asked.

"All good," Jared replied.

"Nice work," Brad told him and the two men scrabbled to their feet. Tom and Jessica entered the open door of the cabin, rifles at the ready. "Dammit," Jessica yelled on her way out. She looked extremely disappointed. "The damn place in empty. No signs that Charlie and Pete have been here." She didn't know exactly what the cabin would have looked like if they had been there, but she was sure she would have been able to tell.

Brad and Jared glanced up at Tom and Jessica. "You two should have secured the outside of the cabin and waited for us," Brad said sternly. Jessica gave him a rebellious look, but Tom quickly smoothed things over.

"We might have, but Lara Croft here rushed past me like gangbusters. I think she would have wiped out anything still alive in that cabin!" The others laughed, mostly at Tom's apt description of Jessica as Lara Croft, but Brad merely smiled. Inside he was having a worrisome thought.

Yeah, including Pete and Charlie. Who are you really pissed at, Brad? If you're thinking it might be your fault she rushed in there like a maniac you'd be right. You're the leader, you're the one responsible.

Did you go over the plan thoroughly, the way you were trained, or did you maybe get lazy and just assume she'd know how to search a building properly? What happened isn't her fault, buddy boy; it's yours and yours alone. You're damn lucky you didn't get her killed.

Brad sighed, smiled, and gave Jessica a hug. He looked at Ving, who was still holding the Barrett as he put his free arm around his beautiful cousin. "Remind me next time to go over the whole plan, will you?" There was group laughter. "Let's get moving again. We're wasting time and daylight." He motioned Jared to the front of the group. "Jared, would you do the honors and lead the way?"

Jared nodded at Brad and the others, as Ving handed him back his gun. "Follow me." He headed southwest and after a few minutes he veered off the trail and squatted. "Look here," he said, waving his friends forward. "Look at these tracks. Looks like we're looking for five men on skis and two on snowshoes."

"Men?" Jessica asked. "How can you tell?"

Jared held out his hand. Jessica took it and stepped closer to the tracks. "See how deep the tracks are?" Jared asked, looking up at her. She nodded. "An average woman wouldn't weigh enough to make such an impression. We're definitely looking for seven men."

The odds were evening up. As soon as they found Pete and Charlie, it'd be seven on seven.

WOLVES AND GRIZZLIES

Day 3 2200 hours AKDT

They kept moving until a little after full dark, when Brad finally called a halt. They had been on the move since early in the morning and had fought a minor battle. The team was tapped out; though, to Brad's surprise, Jessica appeared unfazed by the long hours and strenuous activity. Tom, who pulled the *ahkio* most of the time, looked fresh as well.

They stopped in a small clearing and made camp, each comfortable with their part in the routine, the whole group working in unison to get set up. When all was in readiness, Brad set a schedule for the watch and sent them all to their sleeping bags. He took the first watch. He needed the quiet time to plan for the rest of the mission and to try to figure out what exactly it was about Charlie that wouldn't leave him alone.

DAY 4 0300 hours AKDT

Tom was sitting by the fire and staring into the coals, thinking very pleasant thoughts about the night before, when he heard a noise in the brush thirty yards to his left. Cursing himself for destroying his night vision by staring into the fire, he sensed that someone or something was moving through the brush toward him. The noise continued to get louder and closer.

He readied his weapon, looking away from the fire and blinking his eyes rapidly in an effort to recover his night sight. He heard a rustling sound roughly twenty yards behind him and whirled around, crouching low and pointing his M4A1 toward the noise. His heart pounded and he braced for the expected attack.

The rustling changed to a sound that scared the crap out of him.... It became a low, menacing snarl and, seconds later, Tom was forced to jump back as a large, emaciated black wolf leapt out of the brush, baring its teeth and snarling. Simultaneously three gray wolves swarmed out of the brush behind him, slavering and eyeing him as if he were a steak dinner. There was no mistaking their intent. From the looks of them they had been through a harsh winter, and they had every intention of inviting him to be dinner.

Apparently, the smell of the MREs Brad and his team had eaten had drawn the creatures. Someone had not cleaned up and the wrappers and papers from the MREs had not been tossed into the fire; they had just been stuffed into a box which now sat beside the small blaze. Dominating his fear, he raised his rifle and fired several rounds into the air, causing the hungry wolves to tuck their tails between their legs and slink away . . . not that it made him feel any safer. The animals were starving, so they would be back.

The rest of the team was jolted awake by the gunfire. They scrambled for their weapons and crawled out of the squad tent before Tom could explain what happened. It took several minutes for their relieved laughter to die down.

Brad offered the first sobering thought. "If the guys we're chasing heard those shots they might backtrack and come after us. Tom, stay on your toes, and let the fire burn down to just coals." He didn't feel much like going back to sleep, so he decided to stay up and keep Tom company. Wakeup was in two more hours, and Brad didn't want to deprive any of the others of their rest.

A few minutes later, they heard the wolves begin to howl nearby and soon the whole team crawled back out of the tent to sit uneasily by the fire. The unmistakable sound of the wolves snarling and fighting filled the predawn blackness.

"What the hell is that all about?" Tom wondered aloud.

"Sounds like they've found something to eat and none of them want to share," Ving said. He hated wolves.

"I hope they found one of those guys who took Pete and Charlie and are ripping them to shreds with those nasty teeth," Jessica remarked, earning her a surprised stare from everyone else. She was normally the most even-tempered one of the bunch. Jessica saw their stares, but she wasn't swayed one little bit. "And I hope they crunch his bones too! Whoever these people are deserve what they get."

"Whoever or whatever they're fighting over obviously wasn't alive when they found it or we'd have heard the screams. Being eaten alive by wolves would be painful as hell," Tom remarked.

"Good!" Jessica said, staring in the wolves' direction. Tom began to feel a lot less smug for having shared a sleeping bag with her the night before. He was suddenly very glad that he had rolled over that morning before he'd been able to offend her.

"Now you've got my curiosity up," Brad said, "but I believe I'll wait for daybreak to go look."

An hour later, the wolves had gone silent and the team began to break camp. They had a routine now; it was quick and efficient. When the first rays of sunlight peeked above the horizon, Brad led the group to the area where the sounds had come from the night before.

Perhaps forty yards from where their tent had been set up they found a small clearing with clotted blood and bits of flesh and fur scattered around it. In the center lay the tattered remains of a large grizzly bear, which Ving estimated to be eight feet tall and around seven hundred and fifty pounds. All of them were awestruck by the size of the beast.

"The wolves killed that thing?" Jessica whispered in astonishment.

"No," Ving said, kneeling beside the carcass and turning the massive head to one side. The back of the creature's skull was cracked open and the empty cranial cavity was exposed for all to see. "This bear was dead before the wolves found him. My guess is he was killed by another grizzly, probably a much larger and younger one."

"Larger than this?" Jessica gasped.

"Oh yeah. There are reports from up here of grizzlies ten feet tall and weighing around a thousand pounds. That's one reason Pete loves to hunt up here. There's a record number of grizzlies in Alaska right now, and there have been a lot of trophy records set in the last three or four years."

Jessica shivered. "No thank you," she said. She turned and quietly walked back to the *ahkio*, and Tom stared after her, confused.

* * *

"Today is the day we catch them," Brad said boldly as they began to move down the trail again. He waved Jessica up to his side. "I want you to hang toward the back of the team today."

"That's not my style," Jessica retorted.

"I know. That's why we're having this conversation. When I agreed to bring you on this mission, I was planning a search and rescue operation. This has developed into something entirely different. I know you can take care of yourself, but you're more than just a cousin to me. You're more like my little sister, and I'd never be able to forgive myself if something happened to you. These guys we're chasing are dangerous and unpredictable."

Jessica smiled. "I'm used to dealing with men who are dangerous and unpredictable."

"I know, but my men are better trained for it. I'm not asking you this time, Jess, I'm telling you. Just let them take the front."

"Sure cuz," she replied, wearing a big smile and checking her weapon.

Brad didn't return her smile.

He made his way over to Ving. "Any luck with communications?"

"Still jammed," Ving replied. "These guys must have some serious toys up here. I'm certain they're jamming all the signals."

"I think we are about to find out, buddy."

"Let's move out," Brad hissed. "We're burning daylight."

They continued following the trail along the banks of Fog Creek.

Brad took point, some inner instinct prompting him, telling him that contact was imminent. Ving followed close behind him, trying to keep up with Brad's blistering pace.

Brad caught a flash of movement under the trees to their right flank. It was the black wolf again, leading his pack and stalking the team. Unwilling to give away their position, he refrained from firing his weapon to scare them off. The wolves had eaten their fill of bear meat the night before, they weren't about to tackle the team in broad daylight. Wolves were smart and territorial; this pack was just curious.

It was then he realized he'd ordered Jessica to stay at the rear of the team. Wolves were also cowards; they preyed on stragglers at the back of a group as a weak target and a prime opportunity. Brad stopped to let the team close up.

"It's bad enough we're chasing these crazy psychos through the wilderness," he said, "but now we're being stalked by a pack of predatory wolves! Stay tight." Disgusted, he signaled for the team to move out.

CHAPTER THIRTEEN

GOLD CAMP STRONGHOLD

Day 4 1300 hours AKDT

As they reached the lower section of Fog Creek it continued to widen. According to the topographical map they were now four miles east of Fog Lakes. Pete and Charlie's captors had been in a hurry, wasting no time trying to cover or hide their tracks. Brad suspected they were in a rush to reach their base of operations, and that was why he kept pushing his team so hard.

The weather was warming up, and the forest appeared thicker as the canyon widened into a broad valley. Along the creek bank there remained quite a bit of open ground and visibility was pretty good. Brad constantly checked the tree line on both sides of the creek bed, expecting a possible ambush from either side. If Brad and his team had the opportunity, they would have done exactly that.

As they came around a bend in the creek, they found themselves at the top of a waterfall fifty feet above the valley floor, and Brad was shocked at what he saw down below.

He took cover behind a large group of boulders and grabbed his binoculars for a closer look. The team clustered around him, staring in wonder at the scene beneath them.

There, in a huge clearing, appeared to be some type of crude mining operation. There was a piece of heavy equipment, a big excavator, sitting beside the creek where the water spilled out of the pool below the waterfall, headed for Fog Lakes.

Tom whispered, "I recognize the excavator, but what the hell is that?" He pointed to a long, cylindrical machine.

"That's a trommel," Jessica whispered in reply. "It's used to separate gold from all the other rock in the creek bed. The excavator is used to feed it. It's a gold mining operation."

Tom stood up and eyed Jessica. "Jessica's been hunting treasure since she was a teenager and she's somewhat of an expert on anything to do with finding it," Brad added dryly.

"They're placer mining for alluvial deposits," Jessica continued, ignoring Brad's comment. "There are hundreds of small placer mining operations in Alaska, but this is a designated wilderness area. The state would never issue permits for this."

"So this is what they have been trying to hide," Brad said. "An illegal gold mining operation, probably used to fund whatever crazy plans Hostback and his Order of Phineas have up their sleeve."

The mining operation was surprising enough, but it was what lay just beyond it that fascinated Brad and Ving—a regular frontier fortress made of massive log walls, an inner and an outer one. The entrances were staggered to make entry akin to entering a maze, and to keep a heavy vehicle from crashing the gate. There were a lot of rustic cabins inside, all made from sawn planks from a sawmill located farther down the creek toward Fog Lakes.

"This is undoubtedly where they were heading. I'm betting they have a welcome party waiting for us." Brad shook his head.

"Yep, this feels like a trap for sure. They're probably holding Pete and Charlie in one of those cabins." Ving scratched his noggin. "What the hell are we going to do now?"

UNDER COVER OF DARKNESS

Day 4 2100 hours AKDT

"Okay, here's the plan," Brad said. They'd spent the early evening concealed in a cave not far from the waterfall, waiting for dark and developing a plan of attack. He'd had plenty of time to study the drawing he'd made of the fortress from his vantage point at the falls. He spent a little time wondering why a group that was paranoid enough to build such a massive fortress in the wilds of Alaska wouldn't expend the effort and manpower to keep a watch at the waterfall, especially when it held such a fantastic strategic view of the place. He'd been unable to figure it out, and he had found no indications that they mounted any kind of outpost around the falls. It seemed curious.

"Jared, you set up here with your sniper rifle at the falls to provide cover," Brad said. "Your night vision scope should make everything stand out clearly at this range. We'll stop and raise our left hands every twenty meters or so and wave them back and forth so you'll recognize who the friendlies are. Any chance your suppressor will permit the kind of accuracy you need at this range?" The distance to the fortress looked about two hundred and fifty meters, and the Order had cleared the ground of trees and brush for nearly a hundred meters more in every direction.

"The suppressor affects my accuracy too much. If I have to shoot, there's going to be some sound, but it can't be helped. The rocks up here should give me enough cover, and if the dummies come after me I can pick off quite a few of them in the open before they get up here. By the time they do I'll be long gone.

"This is just a recon, guys, and hopefully there'll be no shooting. Jessica, you'll be coming with me. We'll move up the tree line to the right of the creek. Ving, you and Tom move up the tree line on the left. Don't get too far ahead of us. We meet back at the base of the waterfall at—" he glanced down at his chronometer "— 0300 hours. Let's move out."

Jared set up his Barrett at the top of the falls and monitored the two teams creeping through the darkness. There appeared no sign of other movement inside the compound or out. The only people moving below the falls were the four other members of the team—and there was something unsettling about that.

Ving and Tom did a little boulder hopping to get across the creek and reach the tree line on the left bank. Brad and Jessica reached their tree line first and waited, listening for any sounds that might be out of place. "Are you ready for this, Jess?" Brad asked.

"You know I am. I was born ready. Let's kick some ass."

"We aren't here to kick ass yet. Remember, this is a reconnaissance, we're probing for a weak spot, some way to get in and get Pete and Charlie." He didn't have the heart to point out that, as far as he could tell, the task looked impossible. The fortress appeared too solid and well designed. It would take a miracle to breach those thick walls . . . or an army.

He had a few toys that would make it almost possible, but they were four thousand miles away, in a warehouse in Texas. This was supposed to have been a simple rescue mission. As they moved up the valley, Brad's combat senses began screaming—something wasn't right. He spotted the tripwire just as he was about to step on it and he froze. "Freeze!" he whispered hoarsely to Jessica.

"This looks like a primitive form of booby trap," Brad whispered as he bent down to take a closer look. "Jessica, retrace your exact steps back twenty meters and wait for me. Don't forget to wave your left arm!" After careful examination Brad decided to leave it untouched. *These guys play dirty*!

Grimly, he realized that he had no choice. He would have to retrace his steps and take Jessica back to safety. Brad hoped against hope that he wouldn't hear a muffled explosion from the other side of the river. He would have to come up with another plan. Saving Pete and Charlie had become only half the battle. There was no way he could live with himself if he left these terrorists—and that's what they were no matter what they called themselves—still operating on American soil. They not only needed to rescue their friends, but they also had to find a way to destroy the Order of Phineas.

* * *

Across the creek, Ving discovered a tripwire of his own, and came to the same conclusion as Brad. "This fucking place is saturated with booby traps," he whispered. "We gotta go back and figure something else out. Jesus, I hope Brad doesn't trip one of these fuckin' things!"

He had just managed to get Tom turned around and started to retrace their tracks back to the waterfall when he heard the voice ahead of him. He raised his left hand and waved it back and forth hoping Jared could see him, though he doubted it. Then he and Tom knelt down. The voice was coming directly toward him and getting louder.

SIMON KILLIAN

Pastor Lewis Hostback had called everyone in the Order into the huge meeting hall in the center of the vast compound and they'd been there for hours.

The fortress design had been taken from a drawing that had been posted on an internet website operated by one of the brothers from Alabama. Political in-fighting among the various groups of Aryan Nations made the brother a non-entity for the time being, but Lewis glommed on to the citadel design and the man's dream and had made it become reality.

The major differences were the materials used for construction and Hostback's idea of locating the business part of the fortress outside the gates. Since they were mining the creek for gold, putting the business inside the walls would have been impossible. Simon Killian had been opposed to the idea of wasting all that time and energy on the walls anyway. Who the hell was going to bother them up here in this godforsaken wilderness?

He shuffled his feet, uncomfortable with all the rhetoric and discussions. Pastor Hostback was talking like a damned coward, worried about a handful of people coming after those two spies from the plane crash. The bastards had killed several good men, friends of Simon's, and he knew in his heart that they should have been executed and left for the wolves. If the pastor had done it his way, there wouldn't be a threat right now. He knew he was right, it said right there in the Good Book, "An eye for an eye." Furious, Killian crept unnoticed from the meeting hall.

It wasn't conscious thought that guided Killian's feet to the guardhouse, but it would be a lie to say he hadn't been focused on the prisoners—he was, and he was furious. Pastor Hostback was selling out, worrying about the agents of the ZOG instead of defying them the way he ought to have done. The agents of the ZOG were traitors to their race, and they deserved to die. Killian had been forced to leave the two alive, against every principle he clung to. It was wrong, and it was Pastor Hostback's doing.

The next thought that crossed Killian's mind was that it was a pure sin to have led those devils to the fortress, and he had helped make that happen. He wondered if God would forgive him.

By the time Killian looked up and found himself in front of the cell housing the two ZOG agents, his somewhat addled mind had seized on the idea of atonement. He could pay for his sin. He could make it right.

"What are you doing down here?" the sentry asked. The cell was guarded by a stocky young man sitting at a rough desk reading one of the Order's pamphlets explaining why miscegenation was an abomination before God. "Everyone's supposed to be in the meeting hall."

"I came down here to relieve you so you could go hear what the pastor is sharing." The answer had come off the top of his head, and even in his mental state it sounded lame to Killian.

Fortunately, the young man bought it. He had been down there for hours and he was bored to death. He stood up, tossed his keys on the desk, and hurried toward the meeting hall. There were girls there. Good, decent white girls.

Killian's eyes rose in his head and he gave thanks aloud. It was a sign that the act of atonement he had been subconsciously planning for the last half hour was the right thing, the proper thing to do. He lifted the keys to the cell and walked to the steel door to unlock it.

CHAPTER FOURTEEN

DEATH WALK

DAY 5

"My fuckin' hands are numb!" Pete complained.

Killian poked him in the back, almost missing him in the darkness.

Charlie walked steadily ahead of Pete on the narrow path. Killian warned them not to run, telling them that the woods were overloaded with trip wires and hidden traps. They believed him.

For his part, Killian didn't want one of them to set off a booby trap so close to the citadel for two reasons. The first was that it might alert the Order and bring them outside. The second was that he had made a pledge to the Lord to kill these sinners himself to atone for his sin of not killing them

237

earlier, before Pastor Hostback had brought them to the sanctuary of the fortress.

Pete couldn't see Charlie's hands very well in the darkness, but he could tell the man's shoulders were moving like two puppies inside a croaker sack. The bonds finally parted with an audible snap and Charlie shouted "Now!" Pete couldn't go forward or backward, so he went the only direction he could, intuiting what Charlie wanted. Pete went limp and fell to the ground as Charlie spun around and caught Killian by the throat with both hands. The two of them fell backwards, Charlie sitting astride Killian.

Killian was snarling and biting like a mad dog, and Charlie's hands were weak and numb from being tied for so long.

"Help, Pete . . . I can't hold him much longer!" Charlie gasped and dropped his forearm across Killian's throat, but the smaller man tucked his chin in, partially blocking the blow.

238

Pete scrabbled his way to his knees, helpless, his hands still firmly behind his back. Grunting and straining, he made it to his feet and shook his head. Just at that moment the moon poked its face out from behind the overcast sky and Pete caught a momentary glimpse of Charlie sitting astride the lunatic, who had moments before been preaching at them about "atonement" and "obeying God's will." Seeing his opening, Pete lifted his booted foot and stomped down with all his might, the hard heel of his boot finding its target. Killian screamed as his testicles exploded—literally.

Charlie silenced the screaming man by smashing his head against the ground rendering him unconscious. Pete heard the sound of footsteps running down the path behind him.

"Pete!" a familiar voice hissed. "Is that you?"

It was Ving.

LIFE WALK

Jessica ran out of the darkness and flung herself into Charlie's arms. He was barely able to lift his hands enough to embrace her. Ving and Tom clapped Pete on the back and quickly untied his hands. Brad was the only one who remained silent. Charlie caught his eye and he knew Brad was waiting for an explanation that Charlie really didn't want to give in front of Jessica, but he also knew he had no choice. Regardless of everything that had happened, he had a job to do, and he needed Brad and his team to help him do it.

After several seconds, the team became aware of the tense silence. Jessica let go of Charlie and took a step back. "What?" she asked him. "What's going on?"

Charlie looked from Jessica to Brad and back to her. "I'm going to make this short and sweet," Charlie said. "I work for the Department of State and I'm a federal law enforcement agent. I got involved in all this because my superiors were concerned about a series of Jack Paul's dealings across international borders—and, frankly, they're concerned regarding your team's involvement with Jack Paul."

"Slow down," Brad said. "This makes no sense. First—what about Jack Paul were you investigating? And second—how does he tie in to these fucking white supremacists?"

Charlie glanced at Jessica. "It's okay," she said. "I know my father does some shady shit. But Brad is right. You need to explain yourself."

Charlie shrugged and started speaking. "I don't have to tell you that Jack's been suspected of being involved with illegal diamond mining. When the State Department got wind of that, we started digging and found that he might also be involved with the gold mining here. As you know, this part of Alaska is protected, so there's no way the federal and state government would allow the disturbance of these parts of the wilderness. When we investigated a little more, trying to find out who Jack's partners might be, we stumbled upon Lewis Hostback and his band of merry neo-Nazis." Charlie reached for Jessica's hand, but she pulled away. "I really didn't want to even imagine that your father could be funding these maniacs, but I needed to find out."

"So what led you here? With me? On this "bear hunting" trip." Pete made air quotes with his fingers. "What if the plane hadn't gone down? What then? Would you have sneaked out in the middle of the night and gone Nazi hunting?"

Charlie held his hands up in surrender. "I learned of a possible lead on the Order of Phineas when I overheard Jack and one of his pals talking about Jessica's interest in a lost gold mine up here.

"That guy mentioned that he heard that Lewis Hostback was having tremendous luck pulling gold out of the Nelchina Public Use Area. I knew

Hostback's name as he's been on our watchlist since he moved to Alaska and fell off the grid. But I didn't know for certain until I heard Jack and his friend talking about Hostback and his goldmining mission that they knew each other. After that conversation, everything kind of fell into place.

A few weeks later, Pete and I were chatting and he told me he just happened to be planning a hunting trip at Stephan Lake Lodge. It seemed the perfect cover. I asked him if I could come with him. That's pretty much the whole story."

Jessica was staring at him in disbelief. "So is this," she motioned between the two of them, "all a sham? Did you get close to me just to find out more information about my father?"

Charlie wouldn't look at her. "All I can say is that I love you now."

"Now?" she roared. "You love me now?" She stomped away from him and went to Tom, who rubbed her back in sympathy.

Brad wouldn't let Charlie off the hook. "Aside from what you did to my cousin, there's something more you're not telling us and I want to know what."

Charlie looked down at the dirt floor of the cave. "Look, I understand that you guys are never going to trust me, and I'm not going to apologize for doing my job. When I started this assignment, I was told you guys were just a bunch of cowboys with no respect for the law and no regard for right or wrong. But I've learned that you have as much respect for this country and for the American justice system as I do. Hell, I was even told you guys started your own private war in Central Africa last summer," Charlie said. "With all of your international expeditions, you must have known you would eventually gain the attention of the State Department."

"I figured they had bigger things to worry about," Brad replied. "Our only objective is to save people who need saving. Like you. And more importantly, like Pete."

"Obviously I couldn't have foreseen our plane going down," Charlie offered. "And I can't tell you how much I appreciate your efforts to save us. But, I don't have much time, and if I don't get moving pretty quickly those guys will have time to mount a counter offensive. I have what I need now. I know what Hostback and the Order are doing, and I know exactly where they're doing it. I've got to get a message to my superiors so they can get a force up here to deal with this mess quietly. You do know that it's illegal to use U.S. military forces against a foe inside the U.S., right?"

"Posse Comitatus. Yeah, we're aware of that," Brad said dryly. The others, shocked, were listening to the exchange in morbid fascination. Charlie had been accepted, almost as one of them, and now he was exposed as a changeling, like an alien left in the crib of a human baby.

"There's a decommissioned ELF facility at Fog Lakes, you know what that is?" Brad nodded, as did the other Marines. They all knew the Navy had used ELF communications to keep in contact with submarines, and they knew the low frequencies remained virtually impossible to jam.

"I've got to get there and get the word out to the State Department about Hostback and the Order of Phineas. Thanks to a former secretary of state, we have access to a mercenary force well enough equipped to clean this mess up on the Q.T. They're on standby up at Fort Greeley." Greeley was a little over a hundred and fifty miles northeast of them.

"What about the women and children?" Brad asked evenly. They all knew there were women and children down in the fortress now. Despite what was going on and what the Order of Phineas had done, they all lived by the code that women and children would not be harmed.

"I can only guarantee that the mercs won't harm the non-combatants. You can't blame a guy for taking out someone who's pointing a loaded weapon at him," Charlie said unhappily. "Even if that someone is a child or a mother."

"I don't like this," Brad said quietly.

"I'm not asking you or your team to participate, Brad. I just need to get past that fortress and down the creek to Fog Lakes. As you can see, it's a fucking bastion and I could use your help. If you can't find it in yourself to help with that, I'll understand."

Brad glanced at the others, and all of them met his eyes. One by one they nodded solemnly. They would help in any way they could.

Brad glanced up into Charlie's green eyes once again. "Tell me your plan." Brad closed his eyes and tried to focus on what Charlie was saying, knowing that Ving, Tom, and Jared were listening too. As for Brad, his mind conjured up visions of the disasters at Waco and Ruby Ridge, and he wondered if he had just agreed to help create another ugly mess. He sighed inwardly.

In the final analysis, he had sworn an oath to defend the United States from all enemies, foreign and domestic, and Lewis Hostback and the Order of Phineas fit the latter category to a tee. As far as Brad was concerned, even though he was no longer in the Corps, no one had ever relieved him of his solemn oath.

STANDOFF

Brad and his team were lined up across the forward edge of the plateau in the predawn twilight. The range to the fortress was only about two hundred and fifty meters, well within the range of their M4A1s. All of them were capable of maintaining a six-inch shot group at that range, and a couple of them were capable of a much tighter group. Jared, with the big Barrett, could make a group the size of a quarter at that range on a good day. Only Brad and Tom were not in firing positions. They were down below the falls, helping Charlie force his way into one of the equipment sheds.

"The woods are filled with booby traps according to you guys," Charlie grunted as they forced the second shed door open. "That only leaves the air or the creek, and I can't fly even if they had an aircraft."

"I can fly," Tom said. He wasn't bragging, just stating a fact. "Of course I'd need something with wings to do so."

"The ELF site is three miles down the creek," Charlie said. "I can do this; I just need to find something that will get me downstream past the damned traps."

"How about one of those?" Brad asked. He was pointing at a rack filled with kayaks, stacked four high.

"I think I like that a lot better," Charlie said, pointing his own finger at a trailer that held a twenty-foot johnboat. A gleaming brand new Mercury outboard was mounted on the stern. The three of them raced to the back door of the shed, which opened onto the pool beneath the waterfall.

"Does this seem a bit too easy?" Brad asked.

"What do you mean?" asked Tom.

"Think about it. We know the woods are full of booby traps. And we think Hostback has an army of hundreds. And all of a sudden we just happen to stumble upon a shitload of boats that can take us where we need to go? Seems a bit convenient, doesn't it?"

"Do you think they're rigged to blow?"

Brad wiped sweat from his forehead. "Only one way to find out. Let's go look."

The three men struggled with the massive bar that held the big double door closed and then pushed the doors wide open. Charlie ran around the side of the shed and glanced toward the citadel. There were armed men swarming the fortress in confusion, and small groups of them running here and there shouting excitedly.

"Shit!" Charlie exclaimed as he ran back inside. They carefully, but quickly inspected the boats to make sure nothing was going to explode if they took one off the trailer. Satisfied they'd gotten lucky with both finding the shed and it not being guarded, they wrestled the boat trailer down the short ramp to the pond. "They're excited as hell and running around with guns. Apparently, they haven't found Killian's body yet, but they're looking. I'm wondering why they aren't down here searching the mine sheds."

"Maybe they already did that," Tom muttered as the boat slipped off the trailer and into the water. Brad was holding the dock line, so the boat didn't get away.

"Doesn't matter, I'm out of here," Charlie said, hopping into the johnboat and lying down in the last well by the outboard motor. "Wish me luck!" He pulled the line out of Brad's hand and pushed off the bank toward the rapid outflow from the pond. The water was rough and fast moving, and the lightweight aluminum boat sped out of sight.

"If they're in those woods when he floats past, he's a sitting duck," Tom said.

"I'm not worried about him anymore. If we stay here in this shed any longer we're liable to get an unfriendly visitor ourselves. I'd rather sit this one out behind the rocks at the top of the falls," Brad said.

"What are we waiting for, boss man?" Tom asked with a grin. That was just before a wild-eyed man in his mid-thirties stepped through the front door they had forced open and emptied both barrels of a twelve gauge side-by-side into his belly. Tom was dead before his body hit the floor.

Brad reacted without conscious thought. He flung up his left arm as a distracter and drew his custom knife from his belt with his right at the same moment, thrusting the point up beneath the wild-eyed man's sternum and into his heart. Brad didn't even bother to check him. He didn't need to. A knife to the heart was not a survivable injury. Brad turned and scooped up Tom's lifeless body in his arms and ran out the back door.

There was a lot of blood, but Brad paid it no mind. He put his grief out of his mind and concentrated on getting to the pathway to the top of the falls. His lungs were already burning when he heard the shots from behind him and saw the slugs splashing in the water beside him. The sound of the big Barrett firing from the rocks above him was one of the most beautiful sounds he'd ever heard.

* * *

The members of the Order weren't all lunatics, and there were a number of serious marksmen among them. The whole team was maintaining their cover and total fire discipline. Brad couldn't remember how long it had been since he had laid Tom's lifeless body on the ground and joined in the firefight, but he knew how much ammo he still had left, and it was not a hell of a lot.

He glanced up at the sky, wondering if Charlie had made it, wondering when the choppers full of mercenaries would arrive from Fort Greeley and if they would make it in time. The path up from the waterfall was narrow and steep, and so far none of the Order had managed to climb it. The path was the only way up to the top of the plateau other than flying or free-climbing, and it was only a matter of time before a few of Hostback's men tried it.

Brad sighed loudly and turned back to the task at hand. Get a good sight picture. Take in a full breath and let half of it out. Squeeze the trigger gently, letting the actual detonation of the round come as a surprise. Find another target, repeat the procedure. There were damned few cartridges left in his last magazine. He wondered if he should pray.

*   *   *

Jared counted the remaining .50 caliber rounds for the Barrett. There were not enough to fully recharge his magazine. When he ran out, he would be reduced to standing at the head of the path up from the bottom of the waterfall. He wondered if he'd have a chance to use the beautiful handcrafted fighting knife he'd spent so much money on or whether he'd go down trying to butt stroke one of these backward-ass hillbillies.

He didn't even bother looking up at the sky and doubted that Charlie ever made it past the citadel in that damned aluminum boat. He had seen more than Brad had been able to. He saw Charlie sit up in the boat when people on the bank spotted him and started shooting at him; Charlie pulled the rope on the black outboard a couple of times before Jared had been forced to start shooting. He'd lost sight of Charlie in the ensuing firefight.

* * *

Ving was doggedly firing, conserving his ammo, taking care to aim only at targets carrying weapons. For a group of extremists that supposedly had a large percentage of ex-military in their ranks, they were sure careless about taking cover. He grunted as he fired the last round in his magazine. He laid the M4A1 on the ground beside his firing position and prepared himself for the hand-to-hand he knew was coming. The firing from the rocks paused as the team checked their ammo, and in the lull, he heard the Blackhawks.

* * *

Jessica watched as the group of U.S. Army helicopters swooped in nose first, flared out, and then settled to the ground. Men in black came pouring out of the open doors. One of the first choppers to land, empty within seconds, burst into flames and exploded. Pieces of the helicopter flew into the air and Jessica winced as the shrapnel from the blast rained down on the combatants indiscriminately. Men in black fell, as did members of the Order. Jessica could no longer see any of Hostback's army outside the walls of the citadel. Frozen with fear, she crouched lower behind her shelter and watched in fascinated horror at the events taking place in front of her.

With the landing of the helicopters, dozens of members of the Order came running from seemingly everywhere—buildings and the woods and in some cases, it seemed to Jessica that they just appeared where a second before there had been no one. For the first time, Jessica saw both women and children. While a few had the hard look of brainwashed soldiers in their eyes, most looked terrified. Jessica wanted to call out to these kids and their moms and offer them shelter. But, she knew they'd just as soon kill her and her friends as they would let them live. She had no choice but to make herself as small as possible and watch the scene unfold before her.

The mercenary force swarmed the fortress killing dozens of Hostback's armed men while trying to spare the women and children. It was still ugly, and it was made even worse by the fact that she was watching it all through a flood of tears. Even if Charlie had not lied to her directly, he had lied by omission. The worst part was that she didn't have any idea whether she truly meant anything to him or if she was just another part of his job. And even though the helicopters had arrived, she couldn't know for certain if Charlie was even still alive.

Adding in this hellacious battle and the gruesome death of a man she had recently shared a sleeping bag with, there was no question in her mind that this was the worst day of her life. And that was saying a lot since just the summer before she had been kidnapped and held in the jungles of Africa. Jessica loved her life as a treasure hunter, but she had no idea how it had turned into this.

Jessica counted as every person, both the good and the bad, dropped to the ground in death. She thought it would keep her mind off Charlie and if he ever made it down the river, but she was wrong. She couldn't decide which was louder—the sound of the gunfire or the body count she was keeping in her head. Finally, she covered her ears with her hands, put her head down and cried.

When someone touched her shoulder, she realized it was relatively quiet, in that there were no more guns being fired. For a moment, she thought maybe she'd been hit and she was bleeding out. Or dead. But the hand squeezed her shoulder a bit harder and she looked up to see her cousin Brad, covered in blood and dirt, motioning for her to get up.

"It's over," he said. "There are only a few Order survivors and they put down their weapons and surrendered. Our guys have taken them into custody."

Jessica stood on wobbly legs. "Now what?" She looked behind Brad, searching for their friends.

"Now we go to Stephan Lake Lodge and wait for someone to come to take us home."

"Where are the others?" she asked.

Brad's voice got soft and he put both hands on her shoulders. "Ving and Pete are on their way back up. After the battle was over, they needed to fill in the National Guard on exactly what went down here.

The Guard has been tasked with mopping up this operation."

Jessica's heart felt a bit lighter knowing at least two of her friends had survived. "What about Jared?" she asked, closing her eyes as if that would protect her from any unwanted news.

"He's staying with Tom until they can properly transport . . . his body back to Texas."

"That's right," Jessica mumbled. "You guys never leave one of your own behind."

Ving and Pete approached from the south looking haggard and dirty, but unharmed. Jessica flew into their arms. "Did you see Charlie? Is he safe? He must have made it to his destination because backup arrived. He must have safely made the call."

"Oh Jess." Brad kissed her hair. "I'm sorry. I should have told you immediately. Charlie is okay. He's a hero. He is the reason we're all okay. He saved us."

"Really?" Jessica asked. "But he looked so vulnerable as he was floating downstream in that stupid tin boat." Her voice got frantic and Brad pulled her to him and wrapped his arms around her. "Are you sure? Are you sure he's okay?"

"He was wounded on his way down the river, but he kept going. One of the kids of the Order told a chopper pilot that the man who called for them was barely able to stand and was bleeding profusely, but he kept saying something about having to save Jessica." Brad took a step back and looked into her eyes. "His only thought was about saving you."

Jessica started to sob with relief and was sure she'd never stop. Brad held her and let her cry, sure sooner or later she'd cry herself into exhaustion and he'd carry her to the chopper. "Can

I see him?" she finally asked, sniffing and wiping her nose.

A few minutes later a National Guard soldier approached the men and told them it was time to go. Ving approached Brad and Jessica to tell them.

"Good news," Ving said quietly, putting one hand on Jessica's back and one on Brad's. "Our ride is ready to take us to the lodge."

Jessica broke away from Brad's embrace. "What? That's it?"

"What do you mean *that's it*?" Brad asked. "We won. It's time to go home."

Jessica gave him a hard look. "We most certainly didn't win. Tom is dead. Charlie is . . . where is Charlie? I cannot leave without him. And what about all the people who were brainwashed or tortured by these freaks? What happens to them? And where the hell is that crazy Lewis Hostback guy? Are we just going to let him get away? Just because the government knows about his illegal mining operation now and will shut it down doesn't mean he'll stop. He'll just pack up and set up camp somewhere else, preaching his hate and bigotry. We've got to find him and stop him once and for all." Jessica was getting worked up and her checks flushed scarlet.

"You don't have worry about Hostback anymore," Brad said. "He's gone." "What do you mean gone? We have to find him. He can't get away with what he's done."

"Hostback was waiting for Charlie when he got to the base camp to make the call. One of his intelligence guys must have caught wind of Charlie's plan and tipped off Hostback."

"Oh my god," Jessica said. "So that son of a bitch ambushed Charlie? Where is he? I'll kill him myself."

"Apparently the State Department did a very good job training Charlie," Brad began, "because he outfoxed the fox with the help of a surprising ally. None of us quite know how he did it, but he was ready for Hostback when he got to the call. The same little boy who told the chopper pilot what Charlie said also said that Hostback was waiting by the ELF for Charlie. Hostback told the child to warn him when Charlie was getting near. But instead, the boy ran outside and flagged down Charlie. Apparently Hostback raped the boy's mother. All we can guess is that he wanted justice for her and thought telling Charlie where Hostback was was the best way to get it."

Jessica collapsed to the ground. "So Hostback is dead? And Charlie's the one who did it?"

"Yes," the group said at once.

"Where is Charlie now? Is he coming to the lodge with us?"

Brad approached Jessica and put his hand on her shoulder. "You can say goodbye, but he's not coming with us. He'll go with the State Department back to Texas. He has a lot of briefing to do. And since his job here is done, there's nothing more for him to do."

"Job?" Jessica looked at her cousin. "I was a job to him?"

"Come on," Brad said. "Go talk to him yourself. He's been asking for you."

EPILOGUE

"I smell bacon," Ving said with excitement as they approached the lodge at Stephan Lake. Everyone knew bacon was both Ving's favorite food and smell. He walked up onto the front porch of the rustic lodge with Pete and Jared, and took a seat next to Jessica, whose face was still a mournful study in grief. He reached out and touched the top of her hand as Brad sat down in the chair on the other side of the slender blonde. "Is that bacon I smell?" he asked teasingly.

Jessica sniffed and blinked back her tears. "Yeah, I told the chef how much you loved bacon and he's making BLTs for dinner."

Brad reached down into the steel tub of ice on the deck of the porch and pulled out five bottles of icy-cold craft beer. He yanked out a handkerchief from his pocket and unscrewed the caps on the bottles, carefully wiping the necks before handing a bottle to Ving, Pete, Jared and Jessica. When he was finished, he raised up his bottle. "To Tom and Sam," he said softly. The five solemnly clicked the necks together and then took a long sip from their bottles. There was nothing more to say.

When the beer was gone, Jessica uttered a little sound that could have been a giggle or the sound of her choking.

Brad patted her on the back. "What was that all about?"

"I was thinking about our last 'mission' together in Africa."

"What about it?"

"On the flight home you dumped a handful of diamonds in my hands and called them a souvenir. I met Charlie not long after we got home. It seemed like such a good omen. You know me. I always bring something home from my treasure hunts. With everything that happened in the last few days, the thought never crossed my mind. Just as well, I guess." She ran her finger down the side of her almost empty bottle. "Not much to celebrate this time around."

"I wouldn't go that far," Ving said. "We lost a good man. But he died helping us expose a hateful group that has now been dismantled. If nothing else, that's something to honor. So," he smiled wickedly, "I picked up a little something for you when we were waiting by the fortress." He reached into his pocket and pulled out a gold nugget about the size and shape of a half dollar, dropping it into her open palm.

Jessica struggled with her emotions, finally managing a broken smile, but she couldn't stop the tears. She had said goodbye to Charlie at the foot of the waterfall. He had said he'd developed real feeling for her, but she hadn't been able to make herself believe him. Maybe she just needed more time. But she wasn't even sure if she'd ever see him again. He said he'd call when things settled down, but she didn't even know what that meant.

"Damn," said Ving, staring at Brad in mock dismay, "even when I give 'em gold they don't love me."

Jessica turned and hugged Ving, crying into his shoulder, her golden hair glowing lustrously against his blue-black skin as he patted her back.

Brad just watched the spectacular display of Northern Lights in the sky and opened another beer.

THE END.

Thank you for taking the time to read the TRACK DOWN ALASKA – BOOK 2. If you enjoyed it, please consider telling your friends or posting a __short review__. Word of mouth is an author's best friend and much appreciated. Thank you, Scott Conrad.

___EXCLUSIVE SNEAK PEEK: TRACK DOWN AMAZON – BOOK 3___

He splashed to a dead stop, his feet tangled in the submerged roots of yet another mangrove tree. He was wet, filthy and out of breath, and he was exhausted. Listening to the sounds of the swamp and its creatures around him, he could no longer hear any sounds of pursuing humans, and for that he felt profoundly grateful.

Having to run through the damned swamps was bad enough with its freaking carnivorous fish and various venomous, fanged, and toothed critters without insane men with guns chasing him. Delroy was not as outdoorsy as his brother, a career Marine, and he sure as hell didn't relish wading around in this dismal swamp. Frankly, the place scared the shit out of him.

Damned roots and "gotcha" vines seemed almost alive, grasping at him every step of the way, and when they weren't clutching at him he was up to his ass in either alligators (he'd read somewhere that the creatures in the Amazon were Black Caimans, but the bastards looked like alligators to him) or quicksand.

As if the critters weren't enough, Rodolfo Abimael Guzmán and his Senderistas wanted him—and he knew very well what a bloodthirsty pack of savages they were. Guzmán was the grandson of the first leader of the Shining Path and head of the splinter group in Iquitos.

Delroy shuddered at the memories of the horrendous ritual murders and executions he observed while undercover in Iquitos. Even though he understood that his mission was truly vital in the most literal sense, his courage had faltered more than once during the last year. He had stayed, enduring the night sweats and the incredible fear, until twenty-four hours ago when his cover had been blown by a civilian who had known Delroy and his brother since their childhood.

Guzman himself had gone into a rage, sending his inner cadre after him with instructions to catch Delroy and bring him back and not to return without him on pain of death. It was unclear to Delroy whether he was to be brought back dead or alive or if Guzman didn't care.

Delroy hadn't waited around to find out. He escaped into the swamps north of Iquitos seconds ahead of the cadre and he had barely managed to stay ahead of them ... so far. He couldn't hear them any longer, and he assumed he had finally managed to elude them. He was wrong. . .

Visit the author at: ScottConradBooks.com

Printed in Great Britain
by Amazon

34243651R00160